Pura Vida

A Collection of Stories

PARTS

Italics—short stories

Pura Vida

a pure, simple life

Prelude

I don't remember my birth.

I vaguely remember my childhood—my mother, my father, my first (and only) pet canary. One thousand six hundred ninety-four years erase memories that way. The more I think about it, though, the more certain I am that those years didn't exist at all.

Time blurs so fast, especially in this afterlife.

We haven't been acquainted, you and me. I do suppose the conversation is all one-sided, you being a... what are you, anyways? An angel of Heaven? Yes, yes, perhaps you are. I imagine that you fill most of your utopian days with the whitest mountains and the whitest valleys and the whitest cafes bubbling with the smells of the most brilliantly brewed white mocha.

Or perhaps not; to be honest, I don't quite know what happened after I was sent down to the Abyss.

But we didn't come here to talk about you (no offense). This is my story, after all, and I spent one thousand six hundred ninety-four years writing it.

So, you better stay and read it.

Allow me, then, to enlighten you. No, you won't have to listen to me rambling on about the Aztecs or the plague or the one time I met Franklin D. Roosevelt (though if you see me floating around in the Abyss, feel free to ask). And no, I won't go into my two-century long existential crisis (not too much, anyways).

Instead, I'll condense my life for you. Well, not my entire life, but rather the most important bits, fit snugly into the seven days before it ended. Because although my time on Earth had always been infinite, it was those final moments that had captured me at the points where I'd been most alive.

The last seven days of my life, before the mortality of Earth crumbled me helplessly away.

December 18.

My sleepy eyes gaze across the horizon, overlooking New York's Christmas skyline. It's crazy how much Christmas changes over seventeen hundred years. They used to persecute you for celebrating it, then five hundred years later they would kill you if you didn't—what a weird world. I sit on the roof of an inconspicuous apartment building, my favorite spot on the Upper Eastside, watching the hazy skyline flicker with red-and-green fairy lights. I could sit up here for hours, tracing the smog silhouetted buildings with my eyes, adorned with Christmas festivities.

Of the very few pure things left in the world, one thing remains for certain: I love Christmas.

But today isn't for sightseeing. Today, I have a date.

And, of course, Jeremiel requested a meeting at six o'clock AM, sharp. I check my watch—of course, he is fashionably late.

As if hearing my silent complaint, my friend welcomes me first in sultry whispers, carried softly on the morning wind. The whispers form a head, a neck, appendages, until the face of my companion greets me with a tight smile, dashing as always in a milk-white suit and tie. Behind him, his wings swoop up in a wide arc.

Per usual, he is a work of art.

"Hello, old friend," he says, offering a two-finger salute. "And what shall I call you today?"

He refers to my name. Over my lifetime, I've assumed over one hundred of them. Names are like hats; you can wear them for a century or so, but then they begin to tear at the seams, and it's easier to buy a new one than to repair the old.

"Nothing at the moment," I reply. "I haven't decided on a new one."

He nods, undoing the glossy buttons of his suit. I look down at my own apparel, then back at him, scowling.

"Why must you always outdress me, Jeri?" I complain. "We are on a roof."

Jeremiel glances unamused at the wrinkles in my pajamas, the hole in my left pant leg—I couldn't be bothered to change this morning. "You know how Gold Oasis is. Their gatekeeper can't get away with looking disastrous. It ruins the brand."

The angels call Heaven the Gold Oasis—as if Heaven didn't sound heavenly enough, they had to make it sound like even more of a paradise.

Jeremiel, as I did, led the first one thousand years of his existence on Earth. That is before he died in WWII to five bullets in the chest. By the interference of an otherworldly being, he was resurrected as an angel. And now, he stands at the Gold Oasis' entrance as a gatekeeper, bored out of his mind.

"I don't think they care if you greet the arrivals naked," I muse. "It adds a nice angelic touch."

He doesn't smirk. "It's not my job to arouse them at Heaven's gate."

"I think the old women would be delighted to be turned

on for the first time in thirty years. And besides," I nod to the pearly white of his pristine suit, "why must you put yourself through such agony? You'd kill the dead a second time from blinding them to death."

"Not like I have many choices," he growls, baring his teeth. "I cannot fight the divine."

"Someone's in a fantastic mood today."

"Well, you're awfully chirpy for someone who's constantly a miserable bastard," he shoots back.

I ignore him. "So, what happened? Did another old lady have an existential fit again?"

"I'm not in the mood for your humor."

"I've seen that look before," I put on a juvenile frown. "Did my favorite Thai restaurant go bankrupt? Did giraffes finally go extinct?"

"Worse."

"Did they ban marijuana again?"

He swallows. "Much worse."

I slump, exasperated. "Well, you needn't be so cryptic. Spit it out then. To what do I owe this extreme pleasure?"

Jeremiel steps up on the ledge, his wings glowing in the morning gold. "You are going to die."

I chuckle. "Now, I thought we weren't doing jokes anymore."

"I'm not joking. Next week, one hundred sixty-eight hours from now, you are going to die."

My smile wavers. "Come on now, Jeri. You know how long I tried to find a remedy to infinity. It's not happening—"

"I heard word about it an hour ago," he interrupts, green eyes stormy. "A meteor is hurtling towards Earth as we speak. And once it hits, it will decimate everyone: immortals and mortals alike."

"But if I die, won't I go to the Gold—"

"Mass extinction," he opens his palms to demonstrate. "The Oasis can't let so many people in at once. So, we will be closing the gates."

"And everyone will be sent to the Abyss," I finish.

He closes his fist. "Not so much of a joke now, is it, old friend?"

I blink. Again. Looking up at the sunrise. Unable to speak. "I'm going to…"

Die. I would be forgotten in the Abyss—the dark void between the Gold Oasis and Hell—a soul amongst the desolate wind. A no one—wandering, wallowing forever.

I've never really had to conceptualize death. But now, with my infinity coming to a grinding halt, I can't decide whether I'm thrilled or terrified.

Jeremiel sighs. "I thought I would get a bigger reaction out of you."

I glance down, probing my pant hole with a nervous finger. "What's the point of over-reaction over something I can't control?"

"Were you going to wait for the part where I tell you how you can fix it?"

"And you didn't start with that?"

He shrugs. "For dramatic effect. Do you want to hear it or not?"

The bastard. Always with a flair for the dramatic.

"Sure. Why not?"

He says, "to stop the apocalypse, God determined that you have to decide to keep the world the way it is."

I scrutinize his Heaven-made suit. "What?"

Jeri sighs. "God decided to play a little game with you. It knows just how much you desire your own death, and that wish for your demise will come true if the meteor does strike the Earth. However, if you decide that you want the world to live, then God will reverse the meteor, but at the expense that you must keep on living."

"Really?"

"Really."

"So I choose whether the Earth lives or dies?"

"That's what I was told."

"God's tempting an immortal with Death to see what happens?"

"If you look at it that way, sure."

I scoff. "It seems almost too hard to believe."

He kneels next to me. "So you're going to do it, right?"

I turn the idea over for a moment in my head. There is only one obvious answer. Any sane person would decide to save seven billion people. Any sane person would do anything in their power to be the hero of the world. Especially if it would be so easy.

And yet...

"No." I pin him down with a level stare. "Let it come."

His jaw clenches, eyes squinting in mild disbelief. "Excuse you?"

"You heard me," I cross my legs. "Let the meteor come."

Jeremiel's face exhibits genuine shock. "Wha—why?"

"I have been given the only wish I've ever wanted," I shrug. "I guess it's too good to turn down."

He lets out an exasperated laugh. "Are you so vain that you'd want the whole world to come crashing down with you?"

"Of course," I grin lazily. "But you see, Jeri, I've been looking for a way to end my life for two thousand years. And you have just given me the perfect opportunity."

His face gapes like a drowning fish, the whites of his eyes bulging from his head. I bit back a laugh.

"But...what about humanity? What about everyone else?"

I cringe. "You know it's more than that."

"My God!" he shakes his head of golden locks. "I didn't think you were such a heartless bastard."

My heart thumps steadily in my chest, and I grip the concrete ledge between my fingers. "The world is filled with heartless bastards. I'm just going to be the one that ends it."

Jeremiel just gives me a long, wary look, turning his attention to the yawning sky. "You're impossible."

Without another word between us, we watch the glistening sunrise muscle its way through the night's heavy clouds, waking up for perhaps one of the last times in its existence.

One-hundred sixty-eight hours.

I roll the words around in my head.

One-hundred sixty-eight hours.

Sung over and over again in a monotonous hymn.

I can decide to stop it. I can decide to stop the meteor.

But despite the nabbing in my gut, the dread swimming within me for the mere hours separating me from death, I realize more and more that I don't want to stop it. Despite the queasiness in my stomach, relief floods my lead heart, lightening it into a feather.

For once, I finally have the chance to escape.

So, I adjust the silver watch on my wrist, feeling its weight for the first time.

One hundred sixty-eight hours.

Part 1:

to drinking your sorrows away

A Woman in the Bar

December 19.

A man and a woman, one immortal, me, and one mortal (respectively) walk into a bar at two in the morning. One of us orders a shot of tequila, the other orders four (again, respectively). Hunched over our drinks, we sit there, internally wallowing about something out of our control.

Cause that's all that life is, after all—a desperate gamble for control.

And when you lose, the bar is always waiting.

The bartender knew me right away; I'd known him since the collapse of the Twin Towers, when I'd first stumbled in, dragging in half the ash of the destruction with me (I'd watched the catastrophe from one subway station down, as the towers crumbled from the skyline). Startled, the bartender poured me a scotch, and together we silently watched the replay on the news. Now, our friendship is like one of two old Jewish men, drinking and thinking about all the bad things in the world. I don't know the bartender's name—there's no way he knows mine—but it didn't matter. We are just two beings colliding in Earth's space, struggling through the same human condition.

After all, what else are bars good for other than drinking with strangers?

As for the woman, judging by the bartender's concerned

stare, she's been here before, too—a lot, and very recently. Only their relationship wasn't of two friends; rather, it was of a terrible therapist watching as his client's life falls ever slowly out of control.

I'd seen women like her before—swollen eyes, ghastly face, frizzy hair, fresh from the pits of denial and hoping to drown her sorrows beneath the buzz of alcohol until she vomits it out again. They're sad creatures, these women, but I have a greater worry on my hands.

One hundred forty-eight hours.

How I had already wasted my first twenty hours, I don't know. Eventually, as the Sun scuttled higher in the sky, Jeremiel put aside his anger and got to talking of mundane things (or as mundane as it can get in the Gold Oasis, anyways) all while I sat and listened, my thoughts churning like butter. When he left for other "Godly matters", I descended the stairs of the roof, and I began to walk aimless through the frigid city. Contemplating what to do with the day, I sauntered through Central Park, past Time Square, away from the Empire State building, and before I knew it, I had walked all the way to Wall Street.

It was one-thirty in the morning.

Not wanting to go home, I stumbled along the sleeping streets, my legs flailing like deadweights behind me, until I instinctually found my way to the bar.

A clock hangs on the doorframe above the bathroom. I slowly sip my tequila, watching the minute hand meander across the clock's face. When counting the time, it doesn't seem all that fast. But already another minute's struck, and you're back to believing that time is as fine as the silken sands in the desert, each second flowing too quickly between your fingers. And you just realized that you wasted another minute, contemplating the relativity of your own time—

I sigh outwardly, slamming my empty glass on the bar. "It's gone!"

The woman starts, nearly throwing her glass in the air. "Wh-what?"

"Where does the time go?" I gesticulate to the clock, running my nervous hands through my hair. "Like, once the minute passes, where does it go?"

She stares. Blinks. Besides her, the bartender leans his forearms against the table, gray eyebrows crinkling as he looks at me through them with a worried glance.

"I don't know, my friend," he remarks in his heavy voice. "I do not know."

My eyes dart between their expressions, and the throbbing between my ears slows. I exhale, not realizing I'd been holding my breath, before I collapse, resting my head against the cool surface of the bar.

I look absurd.

Pushing myself up, I begin to chuckle. "I'm...sorry. It's been a long day."

Relieved, the bartender claps me wearily on the shoulder. "It wouldn't be the first. Now, shop closes in thirty. You better be long gone by then!"

Then he meanders into the backroom, shutting the door gently behind him.

When he disappears, the woman lets out a weary grin, pointing to her face. "I guess we've both had pretty rough days."

I glance down at her four shot glasses, three of them already drained. "It must be pretty bad if you're drinking your weight in tequila."

She sighs. "I, uh, my fiancé cheated on me."

I scoot over three barstools until there's only a seat between us. "I'm sorry."

She shakes her head. "I just didn't expect it. I suppose it was bound to happen."

"Well, it still doesn't make it okay."

Her grin is bitter on her lips. "What about you? What brings you here at two in the morning?"

"Oh, nothing in particular," I lie. "The world is just a cruel place, and we'd all like to get away from it sometimes."

"Your sorrow is so poetic."

"I am quite a master of prose."

Her laughter bubbles in her chest, and she swigs down her last shot in a fluid motion. I watch her with a sort of morbid curiosity.

"They say that drinking doesn't make it better," I say.

"And look where we both ended up," she replies.

I laugh, raising one of her empty shot glasses in a toast. "To life."

She clinks with mine. "To our miserable lives."

. . .

I end up walking her back to her apartment. And staying there for the night.

Beneath the sadness clouding her features, she was very pretty. Pretty in the way that stirred up awe, that would get her undivided attention in meetings and odd looks in restaurants. Holding her so close in the cold, I worried I would break her, that her petite body would snap with a wrong hand motion or a too-powerful kiss. But, even ditsy with alcohol, even as she fumbled to open the door to her apartment, she held her ground.

As I sit on the sofa in her living room, her body curled up against mine, she tells me about her life—her past life—when she and her ex-fiancé used to coexist in a blissful harmony. They would talk simply of their days, their experiences, their secrets. For three years, they talked of living out the rest of their lives with each other, to live in a harmonious companionship. They would've gotten married; Hell, she would've had kids with him, the man who she would refer to only as her Ex.

Which is why she could've never expected this.

The night of the breakup, she tells me, was pandemonium. She came home to find her Ex's disheveled dress shirt on the kitchen table and the groaning of the couch on the floorboards. When she ventured further, she found a woman in nothing but scandalous lingerie on top of her fiancé in the living room.

This woman's scream could've curdled ice cream, she tells me. Her Ex leapt, unceremoniously, to his feet.

She didn't know what to do with herself. She would've killed them both that night, would've stabbed a kitchen knife into their sad, monstrous hearts. But she could only stare, watching the new girl grab her bra from the floor and look up at her with the fear of a startled deer as she scampered past the kitchen and through the front door.

"I told him to grab all his stuff and leave, I never wanted to see him again," she says, tears creeping silently down her cheeks. "So, he left, and that was a week ago, but..." she sniffles. "It's so hard, you know, cause the person I thought I could trust just—"

"I know," I whisper, stroking her hair. "I know."

Her story was devastating, but I couldn't bring myself to care. I had heard variations of her tale more times than I could count, and with every blow I grew more numb to the punches.

That's the thing with mortals; they haven't seen time. They haven't seen it drag itself across the floor and burn itself on candles, sizzle in the desert sun or freeze in Arctic winters. They don't understand the weight of their situations, how minuscule heartbreak is in the grand scheme of life's unbelievable terrors.

I haven't yet decided what's worse: her ignorance, or my denial.

I suppose it's only a hundred forty-six hours more.

She traces my chest with a gentle finger. "Has anyone told you that you're a gentleman?"

I smile blandly. "No," I lie. "No one."

We meander from the living room to the bedroom, as the talk bumbles from her relationships to her job that she hated, her friends who didn't understand her, the highs and lows of her twenty-five years on Earth, until we both lay on her bed, shoulder to shoulder, back to where we began, talking about her Ex.

"And we both loved each other, I'm telling you," she rambles on, and on.

"Mmm-hmm," I mumble, watching the 5 A.M. shadows cast bars along the ceiling. Torturing me with this Hell.

I suppose it's what I deserve.

Eventually, sleep saves me from her woes, and together, we fall into a deep and restless slumber.

. . .

I dream of her, the woman from the 15th century. The one who mutilated my heart.

Her name was María, a bubbly girl from the Spanish

marketplace during the Golden Age. And what a golden age indeed—her hair cascaded down her shoulders like pleated gold plates, her eyes the lightest shade of amber I have ever seen. She was radiant, and I believe every man in Barcelona with half a heart wanted to wed her the moment they laid eyes on her.

And I was no exception.

She was a fruit monger, her cart overflowing with bundles of bananas, mangos, coconut, pineapple—any fruit being shuttled from the Indies, she displayed on her stand with beautiful care. Her voice would jingle in joyous giggles as men and women would drop a coin into her hands. Simple—on the outside she was so splendidly simple.

But during the ebb in shoppers, she would paint. Every other month, when I worked as a merchant and would bring my goods into the Barcelona marketplace, she would be perched in the back of her stall painting a new wonder—exotic birds, iridescent waters, the pillars of Heaven—each a display of her fantastic artistry.

No one that simple could ever make something so beautiful.

I didn't ever have enough money to buy her exotic fruits, but I would make up excuses to go up to her stall to talk. In those days, I would converse only to my crew and my buyers—no need to display my horrid Spanish for all to hear.

But her... even when I walked away, I felt like I hadn't talked long enough. I'd curse myself for our trivial conversations—*nice weather today, your painting is lovely, no the sea isn't causing me any harm*—but it would take only a simple smile from her full lips to have me craving for more.

Yes, to say I was in love would be an understatement.

In early June, I took an extended holiday to Spain. At

that time the market was good, merchant life kept me comfortable, and besides, María had invaded my mind and I couldn't take it anymore. So, I decided it was time to take action.

When the marketplace closed, I sauntered over to her, determined to take my Fate in my own hands.

"Hola, María!"

She turns with a crate of mangos in her arms, raising her hand in greeting. "Oliver! What a pleasant surprise!"

She sets down the box, and for a moment I'm lost in the warm depths of her eyes. Like swimming in pools of honey, sweetly drowning me in ecstasy...

"Did you, uh, have good sales today?" I internally slapped myself. Stupid. Stupid question.

She beamed. "Yes, I almost sold out today!"

Again, that delicious smile; I turned to the ocean to hide my blush.

"Well, congratulations," I said. "Are you going to celebrate?"

She giggled, a lovely, jingling sound like wind chimes. "I suppose I should, but I didn't have anything in mind."

"Well, would you care for a celebratory drink?" I extended my hand. "It's on me."

"Really?"

"Of course. I'm taking a holiday in Barcelona and I was looking for something special to do."

"I guess we both have something to celebrate," she said.

"Well, I wasn't going to make it about me. But if you insist."

"What a gentleman," she laughed. "It's final! But might I request one thing?"

I gave her a long once-over. "Anything."

She glanced around at the now-empty market. Then, skirts swirling in tendrils behind her, she leaped into my arms and planted a gentle kiss on my cheek.

Startled, I stood my ground, my heart beating so fast it vertebrated like sirens in my ears. But just as quickly as the moment began, she pulled away, scanning my eyes for a response.

"Oliver…"

"María," I whispered, her name hanging between us in a warm fog. Washed away in the perfection of the instant, I stared at her, sinking in the honeyed color of her eyes.

And in the next moment, I pulled her closer, murmuring her name again before kissing her lips.

Our breathing was jagged, throbbing, between us. With trembling hands, she interlaced her fingers with my own, wrapping them around her waist. For a moment, my heart frenzied, a restless maniac struggling in my chest. Oh bliss, bliss—

But then the world stilled, and she released the embrace. We stood eye to eye, the world swirling around us in perfect synchrony. An orchestra of life, tingling my skin, pulling my lips into a stupid grin.

"Is that all the celebration you want?" I mused.

"Are you serious?" she laughed. "We've only just begun."

. . .

It's nice to wake up to human warmth besides you. I will miss that. Of the top one hundred things on Earth, I think human contact is pretty high up on the totem pole. I glance out the window, my companion's curtains doing nothing to block the sun struggling through. Slowly, I loosen my grip on her slumbering form, weaving my way out from under the comforter and feeling the cold nip of the morning on my chest. I discover my pajama pants at the foot of the bed (I didn't change since my encounter with Jeri), my jacket on one bedpost and my shirt dangling on top of the bedroom door (how I managed to do that is a mystery). I collect each piece, throwing it on until I'm fully clothed. Then, I pad into the kitchen, observing my crude reflection in the face of the clock on the mantle.

I'd only slept for four hours.

I rub the black spots underneath my eyes, tender with the sleepless night.

It's strange. I had been born human. I looked human, sounded human, felt human. I ate with the vigor of someone who needed it, slept soundly through the coos of morning pigeons, showered and drank and lived like anyone else. But of course, it was different.

I am human with a catch, because I have lived too long to feel true joy anymore. I have experienced so many of the world's wonders I'm no longer curious. I have run so far that life has become a song sung too many times on repeat.

But I look back at her, the woman I met in the bar. Her peaceful, innocent face sleeps soundly as it bathes in the shallow light of the dawn. In another era, perhaps we would've lasted, my neuroticism paired with her sound resolution and self-assuring beauty.

But in the past, another woman drew my attention so vividly that even after all this time, her face still burns fresh in my mind.

Leaving me unable to love.

. . .

Fire and fury and passion and love. Love, before María I thought I knew what love was, what it could be. I had lovers in the past, brief and passionate, and for me, that used to be enough.

I was severely mistaken.

That night in Barcelona was a fever dream. We traipsed into a tavern, locked hip to hip, ordering two ales with many more to come. With alcohol to fuel our steps, we danced to a mediocre guitarist, embracing and laughing and kissing. And loving—God it was so easy to love her, the painter from Barcelona, with the face of an angel and a raucous, summertime giggle, sweet and lovely with the tang of someone that knew how to live.

At long last we went back to my cramped city home, embracing so tight I thought we would never come apart. If I could ever encapsulate a moment in time it would be those hours, wrapped up in her fruity scent and lying together on my one-man cot, the lanterns attached from my ceiling flickering like the fervent beating in my chest. But it didn't matter, nothing mattered with her breath so close to mine, the full moon bathing her in light, accentuating her cheeks, her lips, her wide eyes.

If I could, I would spend the rest of my life like that. Trapped in the golden amber of her eyes.

Every morning thereafter, we would awake beside each other, and every night we would exist in synchrony, laughing about simple things that happened, things that we saw that day in the market or on the streets. Every moment I spent with her in the market melted the agony in my heart, her face igniting an internal candle that awakened me to a different reality: one of eternal love, eternal happiness.

It was perfection. She was perfection.

But that summer came and went, merely a small bubble in the great expanse of time.

Only to pop, exposing me to a raw, painful reality.

In September, the international trading season came to sweep me away to Italy, ending my too-short hiatus. The day I left I embraced her tightly on the dockyard. I begged her to come with me, but she said that women like her didn't exist at sea.

"And besides," she smirked. "I get terribly seasick."

"I'll hold your hair back as you vomit into the ocean."

"Then you'll wish you left me here."

My chuckle came out raw as I embraced her tighter. She let out a small gasp as a tear slid quietly down her cheek.

At last, I pulled away. With a quick hand, she wiped away the droplets, a wavering smile on her lips. From her satchel, she pulled out a painting, carefully wrapped in cloth.

"To remember me by," she said, "until you return."

I took it from her, pressing the canvas tightly to my chest. "I will cherish it until the day I die."

I embraced her for the last time, the painting wedged between us. I breathe in her tang of coconut and mango, as if I could cement her soul within me.

"I will never forget you," I said.

"Oliver..." she murmured.

I give her one last, long kiss, one of desperation and passion and so, so much love. Then I left her there, alone, opening the distance between us. Without turning back, I pulled myself onto the ship, watching the dock grow smaller, smaller. I restrained my tears, waving to my one true love as I sailed away, away, away...

How ignorant I was, believing that it was all meant to be.

When I returned three months later, she wasn't there

waiting, begging for me to embrace her in my arms.

No.

María was married.

According to stories from the marketplace, some wealthy aristocrat saw her on the streets and immediately fell in love. He glowed so brightly with gold, they said, that you'd have to be stupid to resist. Within a month, he proposed, sweeping her up in his filthy-rich arms and carrying her far away from the ruffians of the city.

Last I heard, she was pregnant.

She didn't even have the decency to say goodbye.

Every time after I went to Barcelona, I would trip over the shards of my broken heart, littering the streets that we shared all those summers ago. With every street corner, my chest would stir, stomach rolling, mind racing so ferociously I'd have to sit down before I could walk again. Those moments became a string of pain, like someone scraping a bone knife within my ribs again, and again, and again…

I told my crew we wouldn't be returning to Spain—for economic reasons and all. The night before our departure, I gave them each their payment for the week and told them to spend it wisely. Nodding, they ran to the streets like children.

Meanwhile, I strolled onto the deserted dock with a bottle of ale under one arm and her painting under the other. I perched on the molding wood, popping the cork off the wine before taking a long, long drink. Then I glanced down at her painting, the one she had created so long ago, gawking at her unbelievable artistry.

Initially, I hung her picture behind the desk of the Captain's quarters. When I first found out about her betrayal, I put it underneath my pillow, taking it out in the dead of the night and obsessing over each stroke as if it were my last lifeline, tethering me to Earth. Now, holding it here, it's like another rip in my hopeless, ageless heart.

She had painted my eyes, depthless brown and glowing hazel in the candlelight. She had eternalized my passion for her, depicting me as I stared at the woman I'd fallen for, who I broke my unbroken spine for, only to have her stolen by the enchanted gleam of wealth. As if that would make her happy; as if an aristocrat whom she knew for three months before marriage would make her beam every morning as she awoke against his chest.

I will never understand mortals. I will never understand their selfish, grotesque hearts.

I threw the painting on the cobblestone, and with the heel of my boot, I stamped it over and over again, ripping the canvas housing my painted eyes, shredding the cloth into rags.

Then I kicked it into the sea, taking a swig of ale as the water claimed it as a piece of its timeless legacy.

. . .

I frown, reliving the memory. Since Barcelona, my heart's gone cold, scathing those who dare to come near. Now, the palpitating flesh in my chest can't handle anything past one-night stands, and the lovers who make the mistake of coming back are so terrified that they don't dare to return.

I turn my attention back to the woman on the bed. Another hopeless lover—and this time not even with the benefits that come from one-night stands. Once she wakes, she'll be met with the swelling ache of hangover and a newfound rush of despair. But it'll go away. Like everything, her mind will wander onto the next companion, and she'll find someone who will satisfy her loneliness.

I smile bitterly. Everyone will find their happy ending; everyone but me.

I leave her a note on the face of her clock:

You'll find someone, my love.
Now's just not the time.
For me, or you.
XOXO

I take the down stairs two at a time, checking my watch as I emerge into the streets.

One hundred forty-two hours to go.

Jeremiel materializes at my side, strolling next to me as he straightens the cuffs of his suit.

I groan. "Don't tell me you saw all of that."

"Only the parts that mattered. I'm surprised you let her off so easy."

"She was getting over a breakup. I'm not a monster."

"You're letting the whole world die."

I look up at the looming buildings. "The bastards deserve it."

"Including yourself," he adds.

"Oh, but I've always deserved it. Especially today; the girl was a mess, and I left her there to be alone."

Jeri whistles. "After all this time, I'm surprised you still feel guilty."

"I always feel guilty. The poor girl..."

Suddenly, I chuckle softly to myself.

"Done feeling guilty already?"

"No," I say, watching the New York skyscrapers judge me from above. "I forgot to ask her for her name."

A House of My Own

A SHORT STORY

I've always dreamt of a perfect house. Built on the foundation of love, it would be an escape from twisted reality. I would sculpt the walls with my own bare hands, lay each stone and wooden plank until it was complete and utter perfection.

And in this house, strong arms would embrace me as we watched our creation dance through the stages of life. And, together, we would be there for her, spoiling her with all things little girls deserve to be spoiled with—clothes and Barbies and sweet candies from the dollar store. We would teach her to be strong as summer heat and kind as the winds on spring afternoons, and no one could take that away from her.

I've also always been a hopeless dreamer.

Six-ten A.M. Morning light struggles through the blinds, pushing like a child through a too-tall crowd. Sleep drags down my eyes, and perhaps it would've taken me away, had her deep breathing not tethered me awake. Slow and meticulous, our breaths sway in synchrony—mine and my little girl's —and there my heart goes again, fluttering in pride. In love. In dread.

Who knew love could be consumed by so much dread?

My eyes threaten to squeeze tighter, succumbing me to sleep's submission. It was Sunday, after all; I could sneak in a few more hours before I had to face the day again. On the opposite side of the too narrow bed, her skeletal figure squirms, curled tightly in a ball. Off in another fanatical world, she probably dreams of castles and dragons and knights—she's always loved fantasy, can never stop talking about it. If the room is just still enough, I can hear her heartbeat, palpitating as she dreams. For such a small child, her heart tolls like an ancient bell—one that turns people's heads when it begins its dreadful song.

This isn't how life should've begun. Trapped in a one-room apartment with nothing but a single twin bed and the whirring of the half-functional AC keeping us company. Gently, I lift the unwashed covers, letting the cold air hit my bare chest, my bare stomach, chilling me awake. Through the struggling light of the plastic blinds, I search for her on the shadowed bed, my little girl—my little mistake—and again, my blood thrums in my veins. Thrumming, freezing, boiling, pounding in my ears, diseased hatred fuming for the sleeping girl who's become my scapegoat.

I hate her! I hate her! Every pore in my body wants me to hate her, to destroy her so I might begin a new life for myself. My perfect, undiluted world.

Yet my heart stills again. How do you hate a little girl?

It could've happened, I think, my fantastical dream of a loving house. Were this reality not haunted by perpetual loneliness, were my little girl not the insect repellant keeping away the bees to make my garden grow. Instead, it's me, alone, with this creature I've brought into existence by mistake.

A stupid, stupid mistake.

My strangled sob disrupts the silence, and I clap my fingers over my mouth. It was my fault. All my fault...

The room sits crystal clear like the glass that forms from a quiet lake. And on the other side of the bed, my little girl awakens from her slumber. Her gold irises blare like headlights in the morning's dark. Curious eyes meet my own—hers matching mine exactly, but still containing that boundless childlike innocence. Even as young as she is—three years old, God she's already three—she knows in her wise heart. In those enduring eyes, she knows that this isn't the life that she—that we—deserve.

She knows, and she doesn't blame me for it. She never has.

Her too-long pajama bottoms trail behind her like angel wings as she crawls from her little dent in the mattress. I outstretch my arms, and without a word she collapses into my chest, wrapping her legs around my ribs. Her head peaks between the mass of her hair.

"Good morning, Mommy." Her morning breath warms my frigid collarbone.

Gold against gold, our eyes reflect against one another, blinding as the sun struggles strong through the plastic shutters. Forever and ever, we could be lost here, in the paradox of each other's light. I stroke her tangled curls, tucking her tighter into my arms, afraid of losing her. Of living without her.

"Good morning, baby."

Sunlight springs through the confines of the blinds, shrouding the two of us in its eternal, compassionate light. This glow flicks between us, a shrinking candle that refuses to extinguish.

No, it's not perfect, not by a long shot. But at least we have one another to snuggle against. We have each other, curled tight into our reciprocal, depthless love.

And perhaps my perfect fantasy was wrong after all.

Perhaps I already had a home of my own.

Out at Sea

A SHORT STORY

The sea breathes life into me. I suppose it's the only thing left that can.

With the gentle caress like a butterfly's wings, the salty wind tickles me back to the present. Each gust is a song of growing gorgeousness, whistling unsaid words of lives and times long before my own history. It echoes like chimes in the dull throbbing of my homesick heart, casting me out of myself, back in, out, in, out…

My mother used to reminisce about old stories to my brother and I about the beautiful past. While I still lived at home, she'd tell the story of the time years ago when she woke up to find us broken into the baking cupboard and dusted in flour. Other days she'd laugh about the time when I rolled down the grassy slope so many times I vomited on my sleeping brother's head. Her favorite to tell, though, was of the rare days when my father was home from the seas. We used to take day trips to the beach and dip our toes in the sand, and if we were good, he would buy us a bar of chocolate to share.

I think she'd liked living in this simpler, younger time, when the water didn't infest our every waking moment. When they didn't haunt my brother, spiraling him so deep into madness that he left home one day without ever returning.

I suck in a breath, and the salty air illuminates the world into tantalizing clarity. Around the ship, the waves swish in glistening tendrils, lapping at the oiled wood like the tongue of a panting dog.

God, I miss dogs. I miss children and grass and trees and brown leaves at the end of fall that crunch under the soles of earth-worn shoes. I miss the sound of heels on pavement and lace on my bosom and fresh fruit in the summertime, coating my tastebuds with anything but stale bread and the first signs of scurvy.

My mind wanders again back home, beyond the main entrance through the hallway to the living room. I miss the living room the most, I think, with my brother lounging atop the blue velvet couch with the white cushions, reading quietly and basking in the sun's afternoon light (provided generously by the gaping window). The rays would strike his tan face in an odd sort of way, morphing his too-sharp cheekbones into some mystical beast that seemed almost surreal.

I think I miss my brother most of all.

With trembling fingers, I unbutton my sailor's trench coat, then rebutton it, unbuttoning and rebuttoning. When at last I am satisfied, I unbraid my long hair, re-braiding it in a more presentable way. Then I smooth out the wrinkles of my sea-tossed clothes, picking and pulling at the excess. All of this I do to prepare. Prepare, as I watch the ship on the horizon creep closer, ever closer, with the confidence of a beast that has cornered its prey.

I smile bitterly, stowing my memory home where it may never be touched.

Behind me, someone approaches with careful steps. I turn to find my first mate beside me on the bow, watching the enemy grow larger along the horizon. Over the years I've acquired a team of partners in crime to pillage the seas along with me. Many I've sent over the plank without a shred of remorse, and for those who've survived, I would take a bullet to my chest to save them. Upon seeing my brooding face, my first mate's solemn facade shifts to relentless determination. She puts it on for me, I know, to smother my apprehension. But in her eyes, I can see her lurking fear. I brace myself on the ship's railing, wheezing in a final inhale, gathering myself for the sake of my crew who've gathered themselves for me.

It was time.

Our water-stained boots clomp down the steps to the empty deck. The rest of the crew, despite some earlier retaliation, are nowhere to be seen. Good—following orders. The enemy barge has grown to the size of a small castle, peering at us with its cannonball eyes. The castle becomes a mountain, shedding its long shadow over our small, defiant ship. Aboard, the cackling of the enemy crew has me clenching my jaw. They've gotten so close that I can smell the scurvy on their putrid breaths.

My first mate taps me on the shoulder, a silent good luck as she disappears. Leaving me alone to fend for my life.

Their ship's hull brushes against ours, and I turn up my chin, watching.

The largest of their crew, a large bull of a man, shoves a plank between our two main decks. Two by two, they leap aboard, and the ship groans under the new weight. The pirates glare at me like a prize, probing me with their intense stares—a lady pirate, who would've thought? I return with my feline stare, grinning a sly smile that makes most men wet themselves.

But there would be no scaring these brutes. They gather in a circle at my feet, their bestial interest burning a hole deep in my chest. Snarling, spitting, grinning a holey smile, monkeys from the zoo would've been better behaved. I could've laughed at the men-beasts, gawking at me like children.

Yet their unwavering reputation among the seven seas shuts me up.

Undefeated, condescending, vengeful, bloodthirsty.

These were the pirates of Chesapeake Bay.

Despite myself, home slips warmly into my mind, embracing me like a well-worn blanket. Blue couch. White pillows. My brother. I tuck the thought away deep, deep into my mind.

A man of unreadable age breaks from the crowd, his bearded face and sun-strained eyes glaring at me disapprovingly. Despite the thick jacket covering his sallow frame, his spindly, intellectual fingers jut out from the cuff of his shirt like spiders. He joins me in the circle, smiling at me with yellowing teeth.

"Jenny Lou," he sneers. His voice reeks of hate and stale salt. "Surprised to see the ocean hasn't drowned you yet."

Around me, his crew jeers like ravenous hyenas. I manage to crack a smile.

"Maybe not, Peter," I give him a once-over. "But I can tell that the sea really screwed you up."

He socks me in the jaw. I don't remember doubling over. Grabbing me by the braid, he yanks my head up to meet his stare. "I haven't heard the name Peter in years, darling," he drawls. "Does Captain not suffice for you, hmm?"

I shove him away, spitting on the floorboards. Blood dribbles red splotches on my otherwise well-kept coat. "And what made you think you deserve that title, little brother?"

He gestures wildly to his men, the glimmer of boyish frustration and sheer madness in his eyes. "I've got a crew," he spits. "Men who listen at my beck and call, a ship that I may rest in at night. What more could a man want?"

"Perhaps a lady?" I suggest. "Or is that out of the picture, too?"

"You don't want to mock me, Jenny."

"Are you still a coward, then, like when we were young?" I muse, wiping my nose with the back of my hand. "Will you run again at the first signs of fear, like you did all those years ago?"

"Shut up," he seethes.

"Will you betray those you love again, like you did when you didn't get what you wanted? When Father didn't let you play Captain?"

His face strains in pure agony, and I dare not to get any closer. Perhaps then I wouldn't be able to restrain myself. The knife in the inner pocket of my coat aches for my touch, to stab him while I still can. The ocean waves crash harder along the sides of the ship like a thirsty dog. Pleading, begging just for a drop…

This man was no longer my brother. I don't think he ever would be again.

"You're no Captain, Peter Lou," I whisper between clenched teeth. "Hell, Father even told you before you left my side as first mate. 'You're a great pirate, my son, but you don't have the balls to be a Leader.'"

"Father was wrong!" he cries.

"No, he wasn't!" I croak. Tears, stinging with bitter salt, trickle down my cheeks. "Because true leaders don't kill their fathers!"

The image flashes before my eyes: Peter standing over Father, bloodied knife in his chest, as Father bled out on the kitchen floor. Behind us all, Mother clung to me in horror, gasping with blood-curdling screams.

As long as I lived, I would never forget. Could never

forget.

"And then you left," I growl. "Even when you knew it would break Mother's heart. Even when you knew it would break me. You killed him, and you left!

"How can you even be a leader if you hurt all the people you love?"

The blade of his knife emerges from his hip as he lunges at me with an animalistic yowl. I dodge it, backhanding him in the arm, causing the knife to fly. With a fist, he aims for my face; I duck and uppercut him in the chest—monster—then the side—monster—then the groin, splattering him in a crumpled heap on the floor. He rolls over, groaning like a broken wheel.

His next words come out in a strangled sob: "Attack!"

In an instant, his crew swarms me like locus.

But my gang beats them to it.

Whistles and battle cries sound on deck as a tidal wave of my pirates emerge from hidden compartments and behind walls, slamming into Peter's ogres. Blades swing at faces and eyes, skewing the features of those who didn't really have much to begin with. My brother's crew wails, toppling and screaming as metal slices their mangled skin.

Everything that my crew has learned, we've learned to do together. We've grown beyond the forces of an individual; we've become a unit of sisterhood, sworn to protect each other at all costs.

We've grown into a family—a vengeful, passionate, loving family. And we were kicking ass.

Grinning like a maniac, I observe my handiwork. Here were the Chesapeake Pirates, the greatest pirates to ever be born, torn down by my crew. My crew.

Among the battlefield, I find my first mate, looming over

a thick man bleeding out at her feet. She wipes the blood from her hands onto her slacks, meeting my gaze with a wide-eyed stare. Opening her mouth, she begins to scream—

A knife pierces the soft flesh of my heart. I grapple for my chest. Pulling away with glistening red. The world sparkles, flickering at the edges. Feeling at the blade in my heart, my vision goes blurry in utter disbelief.

My brother releases his grip on the knife—I hadn't even heard him get up. I turn, the blood now oozing from all angles of the puncture wound. I meet his unflinching eyes. Watching him as I sink to my knees, blood and bile rising in my throat.

I knew he hated me—I was a constant reminder of Father's words—but I didn't think he hated me this much.

Never this much.

I think of home, or the place I thought had been home. The soft couch, the lavish pillows, my brother's golden hair swept up over his head as he sat with a book grasped in his hands. Then the memory flickers; suddenly it's my father's bleeding body on the couch, tricorn hat draped carelessly over his glassy eyes, the knife still jutting out from his chest. The man who chose not to believe in his own son, who chose his daughter's iron will instead, and who died because of it.

They coexist together, my father and brother, as the home I'd always hoped for. The one I remember from the stories that Mother would tell, the happiness that would swell in her voice at the family she once loved. The family that had been ruined by hatred.

I think I wished that everything would go back to the way they were in childhood: simple, joyous, and loving.

I wished I could still love my brother.

Only as I collapse on the ground at Peter's feet do I realize that my home had disappeared. The stories were mere fantasies, and my childhood was tainted by Father's sedentary ghost.

All that was left was the sea.

The great, glorious blue, swallowing me down deep to the place where my heart truly belonged.

Part 2:

Let's Sail the Seven Seas, My Friends

A Stroll into Temple

For a while, I thought religion was being a part of something greater. I thought that people had created a God so powerful that they could all band together and create a world built for the greater good. To this day, I'm shocked at how accurate they guessed the nature of their own afterlives compared to the Gold Oasis.

But religion is also an institution for the individual, too; it is built to make people feel better about their life's meaning before ultimate death.

In the last fifty years, I've traipsed in and out of therapy offices, on and off of grimy couches, wondering whether they could help me in the hopeless cause of my ever-weakening desire to live. They all diagnosed me for a sort of depression, one rooted at the pit of existentialism. Many told me to turn to a greater power. After all, the way to stop meaninglessness is to find meaning, and what better place to find meaning than in an institution with that purpose at its core? When I would tell them that I knew that Heaven existed and that didn't help me, they would take it as a sort of metaphor.

By the 2000s, I'd gone to nearly a dozen therapists, each with their own egos and not a single shred of helpful advice.

And frankly, I could give less of a damn.

. . .

December 20.

The afternoon streets of New York bustle with nervous shoppers and snotty children. In my ripped denim and snow boots, the twilight cold settles on my bones with unnerving strength. The wind whistles between my ears, humming its joyless lullaby.

And through it all, I hear Jeremiel's hopeless pleas, whispered like incantations in the wind.

You can stop it…. you have the power to stop it….

I pull up the hood of my Cape Cod sweatshirt, muting his words. If I'd wanted to save the world, I would've told him the first day. Enough with the subliminal messaging.

You have the power to save them all. . .

I huff, my breath circling my head like a halo. If God had truly wanted to save the world, It wouldn't have chosen me to make the decision. It's almost comical, though, how much an angel of Heaven wants me to do what's right. Perhaps God was in on the joke.

I check my watch—one hundred thirty-two hours to go. Shuddering, I break into a brisk walk, dodging incoming shoppers left and right. And all the while the phantom wind follows, like a stray dog clinging to the man who gave him leftover scraps. I bump into a woman talking anxiously on her phone, balancing a tall stack of fancy boxes as they topple around her like Jenga blocks. She doesn't even look up as I stack them into her arms, but she casts me a dirty glare and an equally dirty gesture as she struts away. I return the favor.

Perhaps it would be okay when I let them all die.

You have .. .

"Could you just shut up?!"

The flock of people around me pauses, watching me behind judging eyes. I stare each of them down—none of you have anything on me, I carry your nasty fate in the palms of my hands, if you knew who I was you wouldn't dare look at me that way...

But then they resume their own agendas, keeping a cautious six feet distance as they pass.

You could be the reason why they all live. . .

I suppose that's how I ended up in a Jewish synagogue, slamming the door behind me.

. . .

I met Jeremiel at the peak of the eighteenth century.

It was right after I found out that you can make more money pirating than as a merchant. At the time I was in Portugal—keeping my fair distance away from Spain. I spent most of my time voyaging into the new markets of South America, trying and failing to save myself from boredom. But one afternoon in the early 1700s, I came across rugged men docking a magnificent ship in the Portuguese harbor, carrying chestfuls of gold and silver in their arms. Perhaps it was the finery, perhaps it was the stupid grins plastered on their toothless mouths. But that afternoon, I ditched my merchant ship, jumped aboard the SS Bloodhound as a janitor (no that was not the official title, but that's pretty much what I did) and rode into the sunset.

Despite popular media, the pirate life isn't all as romanticized as they make it out to be. In those days, before it was a real crime to steal "booty" from ships, most pirates worked for the royal families as a sort of undercover guard. I learned very quickly the art of dueling with a broadsword, the customs of life at sea with rogues, and the politics of robbing ships (yes, apparently there is politics behind pillaging).

To say I had a knack for pirating would be an

understatement. If they ever had a pirate-Olympics, I promise you I would win every year for the rest of my life. I knew the sea; I could maneuver a ship; I had the dashing looks and hearty slang of someone who never really had proper schooling. Plus, by the time we had pillaged our second ship, I could single-handedly unarm every member of our enemies in a minute, tops.

Pirating gave me purpose, something that I thought I lost two hundred fifty years earlier. I made good acquaintances with the captain of the ship—God forbid I actually still remember his name. I gathered more gold than I ever thought was possible. I even met the Queen of Spain at the time, María Luisa of Savoy, and danced drunkenly at the procession with one of her sisters—or cousins, who knows? Just six months after I began, I impressed the Captain so much that I became the first mate on the ship.

I was content; not happy, but content.

After two years on the SS Bloodhound, we had never failed a mission.

That was until we crossed paths with the infamous Springlake.

Now to say I was a good pirate was an understatement; to say that Jeremiel was a good pirate was blasphemy. He didn't pirate for the politics of it, but rather because he was an adventurer. That's what made him a Great. I could still remember his turbulent laughter as he swung aboard our ship that day, slashing madly with his broadsword and single-handedly taking on three-fourths of our malicious crew. I watched him in awe as he beheaded our captain, yapping all the while about the gorgeous weather. And when he called out brazenly for the first mate, I only hesitated a moment before I stood.

"What's it gonna be?" he peered down at me with a handsome face, green eyes alight with joy. "Are you gonna fight for your life, or will you join the crew?"

I'd heard legends about Jeri—everyone had—his story almost as old as the sea itself. But when I looked at his youthful features, I realized he couldn't have been more than eighteen.

A boy turned pirate king.

The stories had been true. He slashed with his broadsword like a dance, his cheerful tone dripping with an underlying hint of ruthless warning.

A God. He was a God.

I stared him down, grinning cheek to cheek. "It'd be a death sentence to fight you, Cap'n. You're the best fighter I've ever seen."

It was a bluff; he couldn't kill me, even if he stabbed me through the heart five thousand times.

"Are you trying to make the Captain swoon like one of your dames on land?"

"I just say it how it is, sir."

He spits on the deck, and his eyes grew like quarters in gleeful delight. "Welcome to the crew, you bastard."

. . .

The door groans softly behind me as I enter the synagogue. A few old men stand while gripping their prayer books tightly to their chests, chanting a prayer I vaguely recognize. I've sat in on a few Shabbat services in my lifetime and slept through a day of Yom Kippur, but other than that I don't know a thing.

Taking a seat in the back row, I watch.

I never really followed a single religion—despite the peer pressure from my therapists—but I realized long ago that behind the followers and the fancy books, it's all the same Old Testament. Religion's like ice cream—with each flavor, they all just begin slowly melting together.

I shift on the wooden bench. It's not the most glamorous synagogue I'd ever seen, but notable, clean. The tan walls house golden embellishments, ornate flowers that grow into the stained-glass skylight. Despite its simplicity, the room bubbles with a skin-tingling presence.

As the prayer comes to an end, the rabbi steps up to the bimah, a wooden platform at the front of the room, gesturing to his sparse crowd. The congregation takes a seat, watching him with sleepy eyes.

In a low whisper, he murmurs with a leaden voice, "Shalom my friends. Today, as Chanukah comes to an end and we embrace our families every night in prayer, let us remember the miracle. Let us remember the light that flickered for eight days and eight nights, becoming the symbol of hope for the Israelites. Let us remember what our ancestors risked their lives to preserve. We must remember to be grateful for the life that we've been given, to embrace it with open arms, and to always be kind."

The crowd recites back: "Amen."

The collective word sends a tremor through my soul.

The rabbi nods, looking out at his congregation. "With that, please cover your eyes, or not, for the Shema."

I close my eyes, reciting the universal prayer I'd heard a few times before.

"Sh'ma, Yisrael, Adonai eloheinu, Adonai e'cha ..."

I can feel Jeremiel appearing beside me, the heat radiating off him like a fire. With a glance to my left, I catch a glimpse of those ridiculous angel wings draped over the bench. I avert my gaze back to the front.

"I need you to stop following me," I hiss. "I've made my decision already."

"Sh'ma yisrael, adonai eloheinu, adonai e'cha..."

Like a string, he picks up the wind, whispering to me with its song. "You could be the reason that humanity lives."

"But what if I don't want to?" I growl. "I've told you, that's just not the person that I'm cut out to be. It never has been. I just need everything to end."

The chant escalates, becoming a vibration in my weary soul.

"Hear oh Israel, The Lord is Our God, the Lord is One..."

It is a prayer for faith, for the shred of hope that something may be watching over them.

"Hear oh Israel, The Lord is Our God, the Lord is One..."

Jeremiel leans in, and this time he speaks with his own low whisper. "Because somehow, I don't think that it's what you really want."

. . .

Jeremiel and I sailed on the Springlake for about a century. It was the shortest century of my life.

I served as the first mate—his other first mate 'disappeared under mysterious circumstances'—but over time it became a mutual co-captainship. Our bond tightened with every victory, every casualty lost, every story of our boyhoods. Our friendship was as natural as it was foreign to me; I hadn't experienced true friendship in a long, long time.

It was after the first twenty years when I first noticed his unnatural youthfulness—the smooth complexion, the boyish curls, cherub face unblemished by the harsh sun. And after thirty-five years, when his youthful sheen only seemed to grow brighter, I realized that it wasn't just coincidence.

So, one peaceful evening, after another successful raid of a French ship, we split a bottle of rum on the steps of the main deck. The rest of the crew had floated off to their quarters, leaving the two of us blissfully alone. The gentle roar of the ocean wind filled our comfortable silence, settling my restless heart. Curiosity overrode my logic, and perhaps it was the alcohol or the sudden lightness in my heart that finally gave me the courage to ask him.

"How old are you, Jeri?"

He sighed, observing the black horizon. "Fifty-something," he grumbled. "I don't keep track."

"You're lying to me," I gestured to his unlined complexion, his face still ripe with the gleam of youth. "There's no way an old man like you still looks like a mama's boy."

He swished the alcohol in his mouth before swallowing. "You don't ask a pirate his age."

I set my glass down on the steps, musing, "you also don't lie to your friends."

He chuckled, pouring himself another glass. "If you're really curious," he ventured, "I stopped counting after sixteen hundred."

My heart leapt in my throat. I huffed. "And I thought I was getting old."

"Oh yeah, lad?" His musical voice joked, giving me a sidelong glance, "and how old did you say you were?"

I grabbed the bottle by the neck and took a long, long swig. "About one thousand fourteen hundred years old."

The bland amusement leached from his face. I turned

back towards the ocean, watching the gentle lull of the waves edging the boat further into the greater unknown.

Finally, he stroked the fine hairs of his beard and grunted. "I thought you looked young for sixty."

I let out a low whistle. "Did you never think it was weird that I didn't age?"

"No, of course, I did. It's just..." he searched my face, and for a moment I realized just how old those amused eyes were. Like ancient gems, they protruded from his skin, glimmering as if bursting with legends as old as time.

Finally, he said: "You can't get too hopeful, you know? There aren't many of us out there."

I gestured to my ageless body. "Well, at least we have each other now, right?"

Suddenly, he barked out a laugh, a loud, hearty sound ringing across the ship and out beyond the horizon. He stole the rum from my grip, chugging down half the bottle. Grinning like a madman, he shook it up to the sky. "You are a messed up old man. Took you long enough to get me a friend!" He raised the ale to the moon. "Cheers, you dirty bastard!"

And as he downed the rest of the bottle, my heart beat in beautiful euphoria. I joined in on the laughter, yowling to the moon while watching Jeremiel drink himself to inebriation. He gripped my shoulders, something like tears gathering in his eyes. Those soulful eyes sang, joy leaking from each orifice of his being. Hiccupping, he whispered, "thank you, thank you," over and over again.

When at last he succumbed to his exhaustion, I brushed the curls from his cheeks, admiring him. Unlike me, he seemed to genuinely enjoy each day, enjoyed waking up and watching the world fly by around him. How age had not deteriorated his heart was a secret that I would have to ask him. Someday.

Eventually, but not now.

I would have forever to ask him.

I covered him with my coat before leaving him on the dock. Then I meandered back to my sleeping quarters, body buzzing with nervous excitement. I shucked off my boots, undressing to my socks before lying on the cot, letting the ship's waves rock me peacefully to sleep.

For the first time in my existence, I found someone who was left to fend for himself, enduring the pain I've felt my entire life.

And finally, I didn't feel quite so alone.

. . .

After the service, I bolt from the synagogue, the prayers still rolling ceaselessly through my mind.

No matter how long I live on Earth, I still don't know how the idiots do it. I don't know how they have this kind of faith for a God that they've yet to see. I don't know how they're content in knowing that they are lesser than an Almighty being that could smite them down at any moment.

I envy them, their belief in a better life.

I make it three blocks before Jeremiel finally catches up, strolling next to me in his comically pearly suit and pristine dress shoes.

"You can't ignore me forever," he says.

"Of course I can't. You could blind someone in a coma."

"Trust me, once you've been to the Gold Oasis, you'd think I'd need more polish."

I scoff. "Is shoving yourself into everyone's business part of the Gold Oasis too?"

"Hey!"

I dart into an alleyway, Jeri close behind. Fully embraced by twilight's shadows, I grab his shoulders, pinning him to the wall. "What is this?" I seethe, restraining my rage on a leash. "Why are you so goddamn invested in the fate of the world?"

He shoves me off, curling his angelic hands into tight knots. "You think this just affects me? What about the seven billion people you're leaving out there to die?"

"I'm not the hero in humanity's story."

"It's more than just being a hero!"

"What's the point in saving them?" I cut in, baring my teeth at the man I thought I could trust. "They would've all died anyway."

I regret it as soon as I say it.

"That's not what I meant…"

Jeremiel barks out a laugh. "That's the most self-righteous thing I've ever heard you say."

"I—Jeri, let me explain…"

"Oh, my God!" he laughs so loud it vertebrates the concrete beneath us. "Anyone else would think that after seventeen hundred years you'd learn morals, ethics? But no! With a chance to save seven billion people from mass extinction, you'd rather save yourself, because you just want to die so badly!"

"That's not what I meant…"

"I think that's exactly what you meant. What other reason is there? 'Oh, I'm saving humanity from itself.' You think they'll all be saved when they're dumped into the Abyss? Give me a break.

"But out of all the excuses you could've given," Jeri muses, sarcasm dripping in his vicious tone, "'They all would've died, anyway.'"

He begins walking into the alleyway, as if he could no longer talk to the monster I had become. "And you know what the worst part of it is? You don't even feel bad about it."

I brace myself against the wall, the weight of his words lodging into my heart like bullets. "I... you wouldn't understand. No one would understand."

"I understand that you're just full of bullshit!"

I sniffle, the ghost of a sob rumbling in my chest. "I... I trusted you, Jeri," I murmur. "I trusted that you'd be there for me."

He pauses, turning, a dark shadow cast on his unlined face. "This isn't about me. It never was."

I shake my head. "Every day of this miserable life, I flirt with suffering. Every moment, I mourn the deaths of those who've passed. The world destroys all the people that you love, and that pain is worse to bear than the short-lived happiness it offers."

Jeri's forest eyes are desolate. "Hey..."

"When I found you, finally I thought 'this is it. This is why I've lived all this time!' There was finally someone out there who understood, who has lived the world through my lens, and who will be there no matter what. I don't remember ever being that happy before. I don't think I'll ever be that happy again.

"So, when you left, I..." I turn to the claustrophobic city, barring me in the confines of the Earth. My eyes water, but he will never deserve to see me cry—never again. "The one reliable thing in the world dissipated into air, stolen away by the hands of God!"

Jeri's shiny shoes click like bells on the concrete. "Hey—"

"That day, I discovered the true pain of losing a friend. A real friend," I grimace, holding back a whimper. "No matter how short-lived, I would never wish that pain on anyone in the world."

He stops five feet away. Hand outstretched, it trembles, as if on the verge of tears.   "Please…" he whispers. "I promise there's more to the world than pain. You and these people…they all have something to live for."

I turn to look at him with a long, devastating glare.

"The Gold Oasis has truly made you blind, hasn't it?" I growl, unable to stop the boiling tears spilling down my face. "I've been on Earth for more than seventeen hundred years. If there's one thing I learned, it's that when there's no war, violence, or fear, there are distractions—over and over again until you die. I spent my whole life looking for something to distract me.

"You were my distraction. You were supposed to last forever. And you left."

I'd lived through famine, storms, Holocausts, pandemics, wars for freedom, suffrage, rights, money, luxuries. Breakups, falling outs, lost contacts, the ebb and flows of friendships. Dreamless, hopeless, self-conscious, helpless. I've existed through this constant strain of inevitable death, drowning me in a pit of despair.

In 1945, when he made his ascent to Heaven, Jeri understood life's inescapable paradox—people spend so much time sacrificing themselves to the concept of happiness that they don't have a chance to live it out for themselves. It's only until they're stuck in a retirement home and withering away that they realize the dire mistake they made.

I couldn't blame Jeri for wanting to leave Earth; I would've done the same. But now, he can't remember the reason he decided to go in the first place.

And now he's returned as an angel, arguing for the

salvation of a world he has long forgotten.

Jeremiel stares at me like the disapproving parent of an infant. "You don't have to live so miserably. You can't just believe that there's nothing left to live for."

"I'm sorry, Jeri." I push up my gray hoodie, tightening the strings. "I'm doing what you would want me to do."

Then I leave my friend there in the alleyway, launching myself back into the streets. Amidst dysfunctional shoppers and hyperactive children, they all seem happy—because who's not happy during Christmas? It's another distraction—albeit a great one—but a distraction all the same.

I shake my head, chuckle to myself, and disappear into the crowds bubbling with holiday cheer.

. . .

We escaped to New York during World War I, camping out in an apartment together. Outgrowing piracy, we became fishermen by day and party-goers by night, attempting to dance away the fishy smell that clung constantly to our skin. New York was comfortable, and I was content.

Not happy, but content.

By the Great Depression, we continued our monotonous day jobs at sea, but after hours Jeremiel would sell fish to those who needed it, working in soup kitchens long after the sun went down. He was kind that way. I don't know how he still had that relentless, hopeful energy in him.

By World War II, he decided to go out and fight; not keen on fighting in a cause I couldn't see, I stayed home and kept up the fishing business.

On the day of his departure, I didn't give him a goodbye. Goodbye seemed too final. For over two hundred years we'd lived together. Saying goodbye would only bring more sentimentality than either of us needed.

And besides, both of us knew he would be back.

But we both felt the heaviness that day, saw it in the dark rainclouds hovering just above the city. Neither of us could speak over breakfast; I couldn't look Jeri in the eye.

As I brought his bags into the cab, I joked half-heartedly, "don't leave anything behind in Germany."

"Only if you promise not to bring any new friends into the apartment when I'm gone."

"Please, I can't help if the women think I'm irresistible."

He laughed his carefree laugh, but there was a weight behind it. "I'll come back, you know."

I observed him in a quizzical way. "I know. I just…"

"Don't even think that. I'll be back, okay?"

I sighed, inhaling the early morning drizzle. "Okay."

He leaned against the cab, staring up at the skyline. "I think I know what your problem is, my friend."

"Oh yeah? What's that?"

"You give too much of a damn."

"Who said that was a bad thing?"

He shrugged. "I think it's stopping you from being happy."

I chuckled, remembering our night on the Springlake, splitting a bottle of ale. "I think there are a great many things keeping me from happiness. You being gone is just going to add another thing to that list."

Jeri stares at me with a solemn expression. "Well, then, try not to miss me too hard. Okay?"

"Okay."

Satisfied, Jeremiel reached over to clap me on the back. His hand hovered on my shoulder. "I love you, First Mate."

I reached my hand over to squeeze his. "Don't get sappy on me, Captain."

Smiling, he released his grip, saluting me before slipping into the cab. I watched as the car ambled away, carrying with it the only treasure life ever threw my way.

During the War, I received no letters. On the fishing boat, I would sail some days for hours, lost to the thoughts of what adventures Jeri might be on, what he might be doing across the Atlantic. I knew he was fine; I always knew he was fine. Even when the voice inside me told me otherwise, I suppressed it deep, deep into my gut. He was immortal, after all; immortals didn't die.

After the war, he didn't come back with the other military men. I waited for days after, reading the news for signs of lost soldiers. No letter, no officer appearing at my door, telling me that Jeri was gone.

Simply, he just disappeared.

He couldn't have died; I would know it if he had. I would've felt it in my gut, crumpled to my knees, unable to get up.

But gone is just one step away from dead—it carries the slim possibility that everything will end up okay.

I never really contemplated suicide before. I mean, I thought about it—I think most people do—but never in the serious way that follows depression. It was an impossibility that I never dared to fantasize about, even when the world pushed me to the breaking point.

But then again, I had never tried. And day by day, I slipped closer and closer.

It started off small. The temptation of the kitchen knife, the laundry detergent, an open window. I would clench my hands into fists, pacing the apartment with one purpose: to keep myself from doing something stupid.

All for him; all for the stupid immortal man who didn't come back from the war.

I waited for five years, and with every day he didn't return, it leeched away another part of myself. I realized at that time the limit of my own body: I could go a month without drinking water, three months without eating, thirty minutes of sleep a night for a year. I looked like the unwanted gum underneath a classroom desk, shriveled and untouchable. I stayed indoors, and eventually, even the landlord forgot that I existed at all.

I never gave up hope that he would one day come back.

I should've given up my hope.

Because one day, a knock came at the door.

The skip in my heart jolted me awake. I jumped off the indented sofa, and despite the angry rumbling of my starved stomach, I bolted across the apartment. Straightening my wild hair, adjusting my bathrobe with a skeletal hand, I observed my reflection in the mirror next to the coat rack. I looked insane—a homeless man thrown aside by society in nothing but a meager bathrobe to keep him warm. But that didn't matter now; nothing mattered. My hand rested on the doorknob for a moment in hesitation—maybe it was the mailman—but it was quickly replaced with unbridled determination. Finally, I would get my answers—dead or alive it would finally be over, it would all finally be—

I opened the door.

Out of all the things I expected that day, I didn't expect Jeremiel standing there, dressed elegantly in a white suit and tie, sporting a bouquet of white roses, and stinking of rain.

With two magnificent feathered wings splayed behind him.

He gave me a once over, nose crinkling in mild disgust. "You look like shit."

I stared at him for minutes. It could've been hours; it could've been days. I stood there, waiting for him to disappear, for him to become a mirage and melt like candle wax before my eyes.

When at last I realized that he wasn't going anywhere, I said, "Where the Hell did you go?"

. . .

Jeri didn't say a word as I opened the door for him. Didn't murmur a joke at the filthy conditions of the apartment. Only turning to me with a look of pure awe and bitter heartache in his eyes.

He pitied me.

We sat down on the couch, five feet apart with little interest in getting any closer. After placing the white rose bouquet on the coffee table, he straightened an invisible wrinkle on the lapel of his suit, draping his new appendages over the couch. Glancing over at me in the rotten bathrobe with that awful, pitiful glare in his eyes, he cleared his throat before beginning:

Jeremiel had died in the War with five bullets to the chest.

He was alone when it happened—taking a piss in the woods, of all things—when three German soldiers cornered him and shot him until he collapsed in a bloody heap on the ground. At that point, he had only been on the front lines for three days.

When he awoke, he knelt before Heaven's gates, bronze and gleaming brightly in watery sunlight, wearing a snowy suit

with white slacks and matching shoes. He described the Gold
Oasis as enchanting, a snapshot of the utopia that the world
could be. Clouds of every hue floated in the sky in a whirlwind
of unbelievable splendor. Columns stretched in a line far
beyond the eye could see, upholding the gates to the beautiful
city beyond.

And before Jeremiel that day stood an angel, introducing
himself simply as Saint Peter, the gatekeeper. He handed
Jeremiel a scroll with a note scrawled out in gold-encrusted
script.

At this point, Jeri drew a piece of paper from the inner
pocket of his suit, handing it over without so much as a look
my way. With shaking hands, I unfolded the note, and I read
aloud:

> *"Wondrous heart and soul below,*
> *You have proven yourself worthy, ergo*
> *I give you a choice to set things right,*
> *Or leave this kingdom, back into the night,*
> *Be Oasis' guard; or back to status quo*
> *And either way, I'm sure you must know*
> *Sometimes what is right will leave some in spite*
> *All at the whims of your own delight."*

I read it again, the words bringing bile to the back of my
throat. Again. Then I looked up at him, the blood rushing
turbulent between my ears.

"So... you had the choice..."

He nodded, slowly, a tear slipping quietly onto his chin.

"I had the choice to remain in Heaven," he said. "Or I
could come back to Earth."

My next breath wobbled, heart beating in pounding

blows between my ears.

"And... you chose..."

I stumbled off the couch, unable to look at him, smell him, hear him. He followed me into the kitchen, said he could still come down to Earth, but we wouldn't see each other that much anymore—only if it was an emergency—but he would come down when he could, and at least he wasn't dead and wasn't gone forever. He tried to explain himself, tried to tell me that he had no choice—it was an order disguised as a choice from God.

"There is always a choice!" I screamed, my voice straining beneath the weight of my heart.

Of course, there is, he stumbled, but this was a choice that he thought would help him be happy again. And maybe he would finally have a purpose, and as his friend, I should understand.

"You understand, right?" he pleaded, begging softly for my forgiveness.

As if Jeremiel actually deserved forgiveness.

My ears went numb, buzzing, shutting him out. Shutting everything out, blinding me, deafening me only to the beating of my heart. The loud, painful beating of my heart.

Ba-dum. Ba-dum. Ba-dum.

I thought I'd be ready for anything, but I wasn't expecting this. How could I? He had his choice—of course, he had the choice to be happy—and in his place, I would've taken the choice, too.

But in some awful pit in my gut, I hated Jeri for his betrayal. He took the offer, even when he knew that isolation was deadlier than poison, that the world hurts the most when no one was there to mediate the pain.

In my soul, my stupid hope shattered, crushed

underneath my newfound isolation.

I was alone again.

My heart suffocated me. Drowned me.

It needed to stop.

Everything needed to stop.

I walked to the kitchen window, unlatching it with starved fingers. He went on with his apologies, but I couldn't hear him anymore, and even if I could it wouldn't matter. I couldn't give less of a shit anymore.

All that mattered now was my heart. My useless, indestructible heart.

I was alone again.

No matter how much it bled, it kept going. Kept pumping.

Ba-dum. Ba-dum. Ba-dum.

It needed to stop.

Everything needed to stop.

I climbed onto the ledge, shoving myself through the window. Below, the streets called to me. Urging me to go. Nothing mattered, just go. Jump, jump, jump...

(If Jeri could die, so could I.)

At some point, Jeremiel realized my plan. Probably made a desperate attempt to save me.

But I was already flying, plummeting ten stories towards incoming traffic.

Ba-dum. Ba-dum. Ba-dum.

And I didn't regret it at all.

Sea Loch Ness Monster

A SHORT STORY

Monsters don't hide behind scales or hulking bodies. They don't wait underneath beds or roam the deep blue for human victims to feast upon.

I cannot tell you if Bigfoot is cruel, if Dracula enjoys tearing apart his prey, or if these creatures even exist at all.

But, from my own experience, anyways, there is more to beasts than their legends.

As I gaze at the sleepy sun, stretching its last rays on the Hawaiian sky, I rock myself to lull away the sleep settling in my joints. The ocean wind slaps my tendrilled hair, playing an incomprehensible game of Patty Cake to pass the time. I hum to the beat of ocean waves, recreating Mother nature's tune in awful pitch.

And all the while, I wait patiently on the deserted beach for my monster.

Though perhaps the word "monster" isn't appropriate. In the distance he approaches, massive even a mile offshore. From the way his neck rises from blackened waters, he certainly did look like a monster. Fifty feet of pure muscle, his gray-black scales could bounce back bullets. Barbed dorsal fin, ten rows of impossibly yellow teeth, eyes cut like slits, he has the capacity to do more damage than a nuclear missile.

A watchtower, he looms over the beach, observing me with his cold, reptilian glare. A weapon, crafted by the forces of destiny, shaped to be a mighty warrior of the seas.

But physicality is but a shell. I scramble to my feet, cracking a grin.

"Hey, handsome."

He bows as I approach the water, and I tickle his outstretched chin. Where his outer scales are armor, his supple underbelly beckons like a stuffed bear to be hugged. My hands do quick work of his gray chest, and those deadly hindquarters pound against the ground as he purrs.

A puppy. Just a big, spiky puppy.

I pat his stomach. "You ready, big boy?"

He yowls, the sound reverberating across the island like thunder.

I climb onto his back—monster scales make great footholds. I squeeze my legs tight against his scale-plated torso, and he barely gives me time to get a hold on his delicate whiskers before doing a one-eighty turn back towards the ocean, his home. Like a loyal steed, he nickers, kicking back sand with his grotesque talons to give him traction.

Then, he flicks his impressive tail, propelling us into the water, further and further out until Kamuela becomes a speck in the vast horizon.

In unison we scream—our bottled-up frustration and anger becoming a riot that quivers the water around us. I howl, laughing into the violent winds, my voice merely a whisper compared to Mother Earth's hearty ocean cries. With a low sound like a chuckle, my monster dips his head below the water, drowning me down with him.

Thrump, thrump, thrump.

Only the sounds of my thrashing heart meet me down here—a canon in the water, the essence of the very life fueling me. It pulses in rhythm with his as the salt stings my eyes and the goosebumps freckle my bare arms, but I don't care.

Because it's only down here, on the back of my monster, do I finally feel free.

For a brief moment, their faces flash before my eyes—plastic and makeup, short dresses and nasty snarls. Wolves in sheep's clothing, they could beat me down with a well-placed word, could shred through my clothes, my stretched skin, my acne, my round face, with a single manicured claw.

But the moment I chose to defend myself, the moment I brought out my childhood best friend from the shoals, they ran to their pack and hunted me down, banishing me far, far away.

I lived in London before they kicked me out of school. Before Mom sent me to Kamuela, to 'get in touch with nature' to calm my agitated spirit.

Everyone thought I was a beast.

Everyone except for him.

The Sea Loch Ness Monster.

Maybe he is a monster because he looks like a monster; he growls like a monster; he is feared like a monster. Maybe he is a beast because the world needs someone to blame for shipwrecks and the merciless terrors within the deep blue.

But the world forgot that my monster's heart wasn't meant to cause evil.

It was meant to be loved.

I suppose that's why he followed me out here to Hawaii.

Together, we break the surface, the night a chilly embrace on our skin.

He swims in smooth, slow strokes, and I lay on his strong back, watching the dewdrop stars. In the near-silent sound of the roaring winds, our heartbeats thump in synchrony. Idly, I trace the harpoon scars jutting like mountains on the expanse of his sides, his back. Tracing the millennium of hate, healed and torn apart, healed and torn apart, over and over again.

He was just trying to save the sailors from themselves, to keep them from killing one another out of hate they didn't understand. It worked, I suppose; their hate became fear, as hundreds of them shot him until he was forced to go away. Every time he tried to make peace, he was the scapegoat, bombarded by people only desperately trying to save themselves.

He was meant to be a guardian protecting the seas, only to be driven into hiding.

He was destined to be a hero, only to be hated because of it.

But it's not the people's fault, really—the lore was never passed down between the generations. To them, the Loch Ness monster sure looks like a killer, so who's to say he isn't?

How do you tell the difference between an angel and a demon if they all look the same?

Back on the small beaches of Kamuela, I brace my elbows underneath me as we watch the sunrise. He dips his head, growling. To everyone else, it may sound like a battle cry, but after ten years I've learned to understand his groans and grunts as a second language.

'You are the only kind thing the world has ever given me.'

I stroke his charcoaled scales, so translucent in the dawn's light they could be onyx crystals. Absently, I listen to his ancient words plop into the water.

"The world doesn't deserve your heart," I say.

His heartbeat thrums beneath me in an ecstatic dance.

Behind the Kamuela hills, the Sun lightens the sky, signaling the end of our adventure. I climb off his upturned snout, smooching him on his flared nostrils, promising to come back in a week. He whimpers, but I shush him with a finger.

"I will never leave you. But now you need to go, okay?" Silently, he nods, and I smile, retreating a step back.

"I love you. Don't forget to look out for monsters."

In his eyes, I read his sad, silent goodbye. With a splash, he bellyflops back into the sea.

When he's gone, I observe the scrapes on my wrists and forearms, blistering pink from his scales. I rub the blood with my damp shirt, smiling.

Then I wander down the sandy streets, past all the sleepy houses, past the early morning fishermen and surfers, and back to the boarding school, until I'm immersed once again back into the world of monsters.

Ms. Universe

A SHORT STORY

There's an aura around people like me—like us. Conceited, self-absorbed, the most basic white bitch that's ever roamed the face of the Earth. Quinoa chips and kale chips and dieting pills and five-inch stilettos. Makeup and false lashes, fake personality, fake life.

How am I supposed to live comfortably, knowing that I'm the reason many girls hate living?

The media is a soulless demon, eating away at my legs, my stomach, my soul. In flashing lights, as the airtight diamond-studded leotard cinches my waist, the judges' stares rip apart every extra little piece of skin. With the universe's judging eyes on me, I want to cut all the loose inches off my body, tie the corset so tight I can't breathe.

And the other girls backstage, with their thoughtful, twinkling eyes, walking with their natural fluid grace, I feel like a newborn fawn, trampling along with too-long legs and hair extensions. An alien, an outcast, in a world of Photoshop and a set beauty expectation.

And I was supposed to be that expectation.

But how can I, when I don't even think I'm beautiful?

And as I stand, half-dazed from the blazing lights, the paparazzi crowding the platform and hoping to catch a snapshot of my pampered body, I sate my urge to cry, to fidget with the tassels on my outfit, to run and hide so no one ever had to look at me again.

And yet I plaster that dumb smile on my face, cursing myself for the millions of girls who looked upon me and saw nothing but an airhead, a beautiful dumb blonde, and thought that they should look that way too. Cursing myself, for the men who thought all women should look this way, with hips poking out from underneath their skin, their spines protruding from their backs, and my vision blurs, but I refuse to cry now.

For they call my name.

The crowd roars from the stands, chanting my name over and over and over again as they place the icy crown, like shackles, upon my head.

The starving girl from Indiana, who hates the way she looks, whose spray-tanned arms cover the remnants of linear scars.

I am the world's beauty standard.

I am Ms. Universe.

Part 3:
What Happens in War
Dies in War

An Old Man In Vietnam

THREE DAYS

Agelessness bears scars. Not physical ones—discharges are absorbed by my body every year or so. Broken bones are a mere scratch on the surface of my skin. Amputations? Trust me, I witnessed enough in the Vietnam War to promise myself never to put my arms at risk—but in time I assume they would grow back, just like the rest of me.

No, perhaps my physical body will always be relatively intact. But one scan of my heart and you'd see it was all made of scar tissue. At least, it feels that way. If you were to probe it, I'd be shocked if I could feel anything at all.

. . .

It was 1965, and I don't know what I was thinking by joining the fight to 'save' South Vietnam. Hell, the last time I was in Vietnam was before it was taken over by France.

But my therapist at the time told me that I needed a change in scenery after I tried to end my life. She said it might be a good idea to "reintegrate"—I think she suggested a vacation, moving to a new town, studying abroad somewhere, something that might help me, and I quote: 'drag you out of your little depression'.

She also had an ego inflated so big that she couldn't see that her client of six months was getting exponentially worse.

When I got back home that day, per her wishes, I enlisted in the Marines, and two weeks later, I got on a plane and flew to California.

Perhaps God would finally be kind enough to let me die.

I arrived at base before dawn on a Tuesday. Camp Pendleton, just outside of San Diego—a place that I never thought I would find myself trapped in. Eleven half-clothed men were already unpacking their things when a sergeant dropped me off at the barracks.

"Breakfast is at seven," he said, clapping me on the back. "If you're late, you don't eat."

I rubbed my arm, wincing. So, this was military life.

No one gave me a second glance as I threw my duffel on one of the bunks. I watched my comrades, shirtless, making small talk and trying to out flex one another in a not-so-secret game of "I-have-bigger-biceps-than-you." I picked at my skeletal arms—I hadn't recovered since the 'incident' in 1950. So far in the bicep game, I was dead last.

"Hey, you! Little dude! Yeah, you!"

I turned to find a boy standing over me—a skinny teen with sallow bones, his fiery eyes glinting like fireworks. I pointed to myself, confused. He nodded, crossing his elbows across his ribs. I suppressed a chuckle, glancing at the men ten years older than him sizing each other up.

Perhaps I wasn't dead last, then.

"Not as small as you, little-er dude."

He scoffed. "Please. We're the same size, but I know I have something that your little ass doesn't have."

"Oh yeah? And what's that?"

He puffed out his chest. "I have more balls."

"And what makes you think that?"

"You chose the bunk closest to the back."

I gave him a once-over. "And where's your bunk?"

He was dead serious as he said, "right on top of yours."

I held back a laugh. "And how's that different?"

"I have the best view of the house. Do you know how much nasty stuff happens in the barracks?" I shook my head. "Well, my Dad told me one time that he saw a guy punched to death in the training barracks during WWII."

"Damn."

"All these guys in here are scared to death of what might happen to them. I know I am," the boy admitted. "But at least I'm not afraid to see it."

"Huh," I braced my elbows on my knees. Truth be told, I chose a bunk far away enough so that I wouldn't have to talk to anyone, to not risk getting too attached before we set off for Nam.

And this kid just had to give me something else to think about.

"How old are you?" I asked him.

"Nineteen."

"Do they let kids like you fight in the war?"

"I'm not a kid!" he quipped. "Besides, I probably have more spirit than any of these bozos."

Despite everything in my power, I grinned. "I'm Ryan."

"Theodore Wright," he said, extending his hand. I shook it. "But call me Theo. If you call me Theodore, I promise you I'll be the one who punches you to death."

. . .

December 22.

I hate visiting senior centers. I avoid them when I can; how must I explain immortality to those slowly rotting away in their own fecal matter? Some of my war compatriots still reside here, wilting like dandelions in the fall, succumbing to the dementia overtaking them like the plague. One more year, not even, before they'll have to say goodbye.

That's what my life has become—a series of hellos and goodbyes.

I don't know why, then, I've decided to come here today. Probably because Jeri stopped bothering me, and I realized just how bored I was.

Ray's Senior Center resides on the edge of town. I decided to put on decent pants today (it was too cold not to, and I suppose I'm trying to show some respect). My combat boots glisten on the pavement, and for a moment I can't help but feel like the grim reaper clomping towards the white buildings. The center might as well be a graveyard—I've seen enough of both to know that there's no real difference.

Once you enter this place, there's no turning back.

The receptionist offers me a luminous smile as I enter. She types away at a bulky word processor that went out of date ten years ago. What a dull life she must live, I think, to do the paperwork of those being primped and ready to die. I've witnessed her type before, young lives sucked of hope for the means of a couple of extra dollars. I return her smile, a tight little thing squirming uncomfortably on my lips. My black boots drift around the sterile reception room—covered with ugly tapestry and dusty photos of the guests (dead or alive, who knows?)—hands clenched tightly in my pockets.

"I'm here to see Theo—Theodore Wright."

The woman—twenty-six, she couldn't be more than twenty-six—pushes up her glasses with the heel of her hand as she turns her attention from the out-of-date desktop computer and up at me.

"Is he your Grandpa?" she asks.

I grimace. "Something like that."

She offers a sympathetic grin. "Down the hall, third door to the right."

I knew that already; unfortunately, I had already been here twice in the past two years. No matter how much it disgusted me, I just had to see him. But I offer a tight smile, anyways. "Thank you."

She beams again. "You're welcome. Have a nice visit." Then, she hunches over the monitor again, type, typing away.

I don't even have room to pity her.

I leave her there in the dust of her deteriorating young life. With trepidation in my gut, I venture into the labyrinth of sterile rooms housing the dying lives of the old.

. . .

During my three months at Camp Pendleton, I learned three things:

One, compared to the men in my barracks, I was severely out of shape.

The first four weeks of basic training consisted of screening procedures: doctor's reports, weapon handling, a crash course to the Marines. This got me too comfortable, too self-assured that the military would be a walk in the park.

Then week five kicked me in the ass.

Turns out, running five miles on the beach is a military warm-up. In the first week of our second stage of training, I could barely do a mile before my lungs seared like barbeque and I vomited up dinner from the night before. Theo didn't fare much better, but unlike me, he had the decency not to puke out all his innards (or if he did, I never saw him do it). The sergeant overseeing our training assigned the two of us to after-hours running practice, so that maybe before wartime we would actually stand a chance of surviving in South Vietnam.

I think he was trying to be encouraging.

In other areas, my arm strength was near non-existent. After giving me a long, pained look, our drill sergeant started me off on 'assisted pushups' —a euphemism for 'exercises-for-men-that-seven-year-old-children-could-do', and on my first day, I completed ten (technically eight, but I didn't need to be more humiliated than I already was). I couldn't do a pull-up—even after the first week. All I could muster was a swift grunt and an ungraceful drop from the bar.

And the assault training? The Drills? Forget about it. My heart was so burnt out from the morning's cardio that I felt like I was walking up an uphill railroad track for the rest of the day.

Every night, I collapsed onto the bunk; each morning, it took iron willpower that I didn't know I had to lift myself from the bed. Each day, the world kicked me in the gut and landed ten punches to my face before I was even conscious enough to open my eyes. It was a blessing that I even woke up early enough to get breakfast at all (the sergeant was right—by seven o' one the cooks dismissed the late folk with vulgar gestures).

One thing I killed, though (no pun intended): marksmanship. On the fifth day of the second phase, they shuttled the lot of us to the far end of camp and onto Edson Range, a vast dust field lined with human cutouts as targets, standing ominously in a row. We took turns firing—laid on our stomach or kneeled on the ground—and when the rotation came around to me, I didn't hesitate before I rolled onto my torso, pointed the barrel of my gun at the target, and shot.

Bang!

Bang!

Bang!

I had nailed three bullets dead-on into the cutout's chest.

My aim was deadly accurate, and by the end of the day, all my barrack-mates gathered around as they watched me at work. They cheered for the "little man", clapping and whooping as I hit my thirtieth bullseye in a row.

As we cleaned up, Theo sauntered over to me and asked, "how'd you get so good at that?"

I shrugged, silently thanking my time wielding muskets at sea. "I can't be shit at everything, right?"

Two, camp life wasn't all as bad as Theo's dad made it out to be.

After the godawful fifth week, another soldier in my barrack—Bruce, dubbed by the Sergeant as the 'Marines prodigy' —swaggered up to my bunk. "Hey, little man!"

I looked up from my book. "Hey...big man!"

"You're some shot, huh?"

"Yeah, I guess I am." I braced myself for a fist to the face.

Instead, he rubbed the back of his meat-block head and said: "I want you to teach me."

"What?"

"Look, man," he said. "I'm a bad shot, and I need someone like you to teach me."

I eyed him warily. "What's the catch?"

"Man, it's not like that!" he grabbed my shoulder with a gorilla hand. "I wanna get my shot better, alright? I'll do anything. Please."

I looked into his eyes, and despite his hulking form, his face pleaded like a puppy's, wide and hopeful. Innocent. Every instinct told me to cower, to deny him and survive the rest of my time in the military in my own isolation.

But he was no killer; he had no fighting instinct to survive. He was just a boy in a lethal body who wanted my help.

Perhaps my sympathy will be the death of me one day.

I sighed. "I'll teach you. But on one condition: get Theo and me in shape before Nam."

Bruce let out a relieved laugh. "That's it? I can do that!"

I held out a scrawny hand, offering a weak smile. "Then you got yourself a deal."

He broke into a toothy grin, grabbing my fingers in a bone-breaking grip. "Glad to do business with you, little man."

And so it began.

During lunchtime, Bruce and I would take our sandwiches to the range, and I adjusted his awkward form as he fired shots.

"Aim a little bit higher...now make sure your elbow is by your ear...shift to the left—your other left!"

He missed the target by three feet.

"Hey don't worry," I clapped him on the back. "You'll get it next time."

He truly was terrible—and in my time I'd seen some terrible shots.

After dinnertime, Bruce took Theo and me out to the fields, drilling us on sprints, jumping jacks, getting down and giving him ten.

"Is that all you got, little man?"

I was always too exhausted to respond.

But we all got better. By week eight I could get through

the five miles with only mild discomfort; Bruce could (almost) hit the target every three shots; Theo could make it through seven 'real' pushups when the sergeant asked him to do ten.

Over time, it got easier, and my bunkmates seemed to notice. "Lookin' good, little man! You're getting your shoulders now! Not so little anymore, are ya?"

I smiled, I cracked jokes, I even challenged one of the big guys, Luke, to an arm-wrestling fight (if Bruce hadn't stepped in, I think I would've lost an arm.)

But I always kept up my carefully crafted wall. After dark, I would make up excuses to go back to the bunks, if only to deflect new friendships. I wasn't ready to make any more 'true' friends, not yet.

Which is what made Theo so goddamn annoying.

Three, no matter how much I tried, I couldn't dislike Theo.

And trust me, I really tried.

From week one, he wouldn't leave my side. Even as I gave him the cold shoulder during our screenings, even as I sat as humanely far away from him during mealtimes as I could, he stuck like a magnet with no intention of letting go. Eventually, avoidance became tolerance, and I learned to put up with his nearly unbearable rambling.

God, that kid talked like his life depended on it. Like he would implode if he couldn't make that one backhanded comment. It drove me insane.

For the first six weeks, he came up to me every day with a new set of questions, drilling me all throughout the morning run, breakfast, formations.

"Where are you from, Ryan?"

"Doesn't matter."

"Why are you in the military now, huh?"

"Cause I wanted to."

"Why are you so quiet all the time?"

I didn't respond to that one.

"You're really an ass, you know that?"

I couldn't avoid him—he was my bunk buddy—so I did my best deflecting his questions or just not answering them at all. "Ooh, so mysterious," he mused constantly. "Maybe you're a magician, that's why you don't want to show me any of your tricks."

"Keep running your mouth and I'll turn you into a rabbit."

But I liked him, probably more than I should've. For a kid with a mouth the size of Jupiter, I was surprised to find there was enough room for a good brain in his chatterbox skull. By the seventh week, he mostly gave up on trying to figure me out and turned towards spilling his own guts instead. He told me that he wanted to be a part of the space race when he got out of high school. Applied for a NASA scholarship and everything. When Theo came home from his senior year graduation, a bag was already packed for the military, lying there against the doorframe. His father told him that he enlisted his son in the Marines so that he could 'learn to be a real man'.

Theo's acceptance letter laid, ripped open, on the kitchen counter.

"Dad didn't want me building spaceships," he told me over dinner, chuckling. No matter what, he could always laugh. "Didn't think that it's a real job."

"I think your dad's an idiot."

Maybe it was a part of being bunkmates, maybe because we were the most unathletic people in camp, maybe because I was the only one who could put up with his rambling, but against my will, we became inseparable. Against my will, I eventually opened up—nothing all too special, just some selected stories about my recent job, my few memories of childhood, my favorite pastries from France.

But I didn't tell him everything—beyond Jeri, I kept my immortality a secret. As far as Theo was concerned, I was a twenty-one-year-old fisherman from New York City looking to serve the country.

I made acquaintances with my bunkmates. I was in the best shape of my life. For a moment—a stupid, pitiful moment—I wondered if going to war was even so bad after all. Even into the final stages of Water Survival Training and the godawful Crucible, I survived. We survived, and our bunkmates became closer because of it.

Naively, we were all fooled into thinking the war would be a piece of cake.

Then they flew us to Vietnam.

. . .

When I enter the room, Theo sits in his wheelchair facing the window, watching the outside with a gentle bobbing of his frail head. I don't say a word, don't get a good look at him, merely cross the room and sit cross-legged on the floor beside him. He cast me a sidelong glance before returning his gaze to the robin on the outside windowsill.

"I thought immortal bastards don't visit senior homes."

That's always his opening line after I told him the same thing the first time I came to visit.

"I make exceptions."

His laughter rumbles like distant thunder in his chest. "I'm so flattered to be worthy of your visits to my death bed."

"Well, they could've at least picked some nicer curtains. What the Hell were they thinking?"

His eyes traverse the plain white room, adorned with tan curtains, tan light shades, tan covers on the quaint, sterile bed. "It doesn't matter how it looks, I guess. I'm not an Egyptian king or anything."

Every time, this was our opening conversation, neither of us able to confront the elephant in the room:

Theo is dying.

I refuse to look at him. Refuse to accept the mortality of his strong voice, stronger mind. The last couple of times I visited, I refused to sit anywhere but sideways to him, averting my gaze so I wouldn't ever be in the position to look at him. And yet I feel his stare on my youthful countenance, prodding me, pleading with me. He knew what I was doing, and it killed him.

When at last the tension became too great, I say: "Screw this place. I'll make a nice place for you in my apartment, and I'll fill it with whatever the Hell you want. Would you be more at peace there?"

His breath catches as the robin on the other side of the glass sings sweetly before returning to the sky. The vast, euphoric sky. "And what happens when I finally die?"

I shrug nonchalantly. "I'll put a rug over you, and I'll never mention your existence again. The only problem is that I have to deal with the smell of your carcass, but I'll make do."

His chuckle rumbles more surely now, igniting a spark in his faulty chest. "Wouldn't I love that?"

"Would you rather me crucify you?"

"If you do, make it public," he says. "And I want you to

take a butcher knife, and I want everyone to witness my cold naked body as my intestines spill out."

I shudder. "Never in my seventeen hundred years have I ever heard something so horrific."

"I'm flattered."

I look at his shorts, hideous khakis displaying his stick legs with blue, car cable veins snaking through his skin. I turn my attention quickly back to the window. "Don't be so cocky about it. It wasn't meant to be a compliment."

"Why not? I made an immortal squirm; that's something worth celebrating."

"You are a spineless, egotistical old man."

He cackles, a youthful sound, crackling like lightning. "If they crucify me, does that mean I'll go to Heaven?"

"Does it matter where we go?"

"Maybe for you it doesn't." I feel his blue irises burning a hole in my scalp. His eyes are the only lasting evidence of who he used to be, two probing spheres peeking from beneath a sagging face. Even with age, his intensity never went away. "But for me, I can't help but wonder, you know? Maybe it's wishful thinking to think I'd live forever, but maybe it's just for the best that I don't. I know you don't care, but would you want Heaven to exist?"

"I... I don't know." Out of everything I've told him, I never said a word about the Gold Oasis. I would never dare give that information to anyone in the world.

His eyes—fiery, sapphire eyes stronger than the adversity he faced in Vietnam—ever prod, ever bore through me. Besides me, I hear him scoff. "I thought you were stronger than that."

"Stronger than what?"

"That after all these years, after everything you've seen,

you'd finally be able to face death."

"Who says I haven't?"

"Because you still won't look at me."

And there was the elephant.

My heart thumps, loudly, in my ears. "Yeah, so? Doesn't mean I'm afraid"

"So?" he mocks. "You can't even look at me without thinking about the fact that I'm going to die!"

"Stop saying that—"

You're so worried about hurting yourself that you can't even face what's happening right in front of you."

"You're wrong!"

"You're still a child, you know that? You can't stop indulging this fantasy that everything will turn out the way you want it to!"

My heart skips, breath stifling. "Am I a child to not want to watch any more people die?"

"You're afraid," he growls. "Afraid of losing what you love, and you deal with that fear by pretending it doesn't exist. Sounds childish to me."

"It's not that simple—"

"How am I supposed to die peacefully if my best friend can't even look me in the face on my deathbed?" he fumes, pain icing his words with a quiet fury. "Look at me."

"No, Theo—"

"You old, impenetrable bastard. Look at me. In the grand scheme of things, I don't even matter."

"That's not true."

"Just look at me, Ryan!"

"Theo, stop—"

"I am dying, Ryan! And you're just going to leave me like this before I die—"

"Fine!" I scream. "Fine! Just...shut up."

Theo's ironclad stubbornness—the one thing I both admire and hate about him.

"Thank you," he murmurs, so quiet his words could've been a figment of my imagination.

I stand, squeezing my eyes shut.

"You can't just hope that I'll disappear," he whispers.

I remember what he said in camp that first day— 'All these guys in here are scared to death of what might happen to them, but at least I'm not afraid to see it.'

"I don't know how you've spent your entire life unafraid to see the world the way it is," I breathe.

"Learn something from your old man, then," Theo grumbles.

I inhale.

Exhale.

And, slowly, I look.

. . .

Nothing could prepare me for the war. The vulgar, heart-wrenching war.

On July eleventh, 1965, Theo and I landed in the tropical terrain of our jungle camp. Even on mild days, the base steamed with sweat and hot mist. And on most days, the blistering heat gnawed at uslike the mosquitoes who bit us relentlessly. Even in camp, we couldn't relax from the constant tension and ever-looming presence of death lurking just beyond the perimeter.

In the first two weeks, ten of the twenty-five hundred men in camp fell ill from heat stroke. As we paraded like prized cows through the Vietnamese jungles, scouting out the land that the front line left behind, many more collapsed from various tropical diseases. Even before the fighting began, so many succumbed to the environment that I began to question who we were really fighting a war against.

That was when the first battle began in November in the Ia Drang Valley.

I wasn't there; no one in my battalion was, but it lodged fear in our hearts all the same. Finally—finally—a real battle had come, and we had won.

We had won, and yet so many of us had died.

I don't know much about military strategy; they attempted to teach us during training, but in times of war and adrenaline I couldn't do much but follow orders from the nearest Sergeant and aim at the opposite side. I suppose that's the best I could do. War was following commands, and I worried that if I thought about it too much, I wouldn't dare get out of my sleeping bag in the morning.

Every night, I would come back to a base bubbling with gossip about the day. Occasionally, the soldiers would speak of surprise ambushes, other times unexpected shootouts. The leaders at camp assured us that not many of us would die—the chance of a surprise attack was so small that the chance of it happening was as likely as us dying back in the States.

"Liars," Theo mutters under his breath.

As usual, he was right.

Every moment was laced with uncertainty, and every day life was a blessing sent down by merciful fate. Theo and I were quickly separated from our old barrack mates, but by some will of God, we were always kept together. Even in times of reassignment, Theo always managed to find his way back to me somehow.

And even though my fate was secured in the folds of

chance...I hated to admit it, but I couldn't stand the idea of losing Theo.

Not like I would ever tell the bastard.

January fifth, 1966. It was ten in the morning, and sweat gathered in large pools underneath my uniform as one hundred of us marched through the jungle scouting out the new area. Theo trotted beside me, shouldering his rifle with a poise he didn't have nine months ago. He'd put on some muscle—albeit all of us did, too—his newfound maturity creasing his forehead with stress marks. If I hadn't known better, I would've said that the military had hardened him, shaped him into the man that his father wanted him to become.

But then he glanced over his shoulder at me, sticking out his tongue and waggling his eyebrows. I suppressed my grin.

Oh, he was still Theo on the inside—snarky, intelligent Theo.

Bam!

Our fleet stopped, cocking our guns to all sides of the forest.

The birds in the trees scattered with a shrieking caw.

We stilled,

waiting for the next attack.

I stole a glance at Theo,

his crystal eyes darting through the trees,

then to me.

Afraid.

Determined,

but afraid.

I inhaled.

Exhaled.

Breathe.

Bam!

Bam!

The men in the front crumpled to the ground. Like cockroaches, the rest of us dropped to our knees and scuttled for cover.

It was an ambush, and the Second Lieutenant leading our company hadn't seen it coming.

Around me, men collapsed in waves. I ducked down beneath the roots of a large tree, pressing my back against it for dear life. Though I couldn't see the Viet-Cong enemy, their damage was extraordinary, taking down three, five, seven of our soldiers...

Our men's lives extinguished like water on campfires. Down, just like that.

My breath sputtered like a car running out of gasoline as I peeked out from behind my tree, firing blindly out at the enemy. A grunt and a curse later, a man collapsed to the ground.

He was the Viet Cong's first casualty.

My heart galloped in my chest.

I had killed a man.

And though it wasn't my first murder, it raked terror through me all the same.

Cradling my rifle to my chest, I played a dangerous game of peek-a-boo, bullets flying past my head as I ducked back into my hiding spot. Shoot, pull back. Shoot, pull back. Adrenaline flooded me like a typhoon, wiring my body taut as I kept shooting, cowering, aiming, hiding.

Afraid.

I shouldn't have been so goddamn afraid.

Because I had nothing to be afraid of. Death didn't scare me, I thought. I fired another shot, pinpointing the scream attached to it, yowling in agony before taking his final breath. My back pressed against the tree trunk as I cradled my rifle like a newborn. Behind me, I heard the gunshots, the hollow cries of soldiers, the pain of a war that didn't need to be fought.

And through it all, someone called my name.

"Ryan? Ryan!"

Theo.

I peered out from behind my hiding spot, and there, like a deer in the headlights, he glanced around frantically, crying: "Ryan!"

Out in the open, he stepped over the dead bodies of his comrades, his voice raw from screaming. Looking for me.

That goddamn idiot.

I ran out from behind my tree, leaping for him. I tackled him to the ground, shushing him with my bloodied finger—why was I bleeding?

His sharp eyes watered as he stared up at me in blind wonder. "Ryan?"

I punched him in the jaw.

"You idiot!" I roared. "What the Hell were you thinking—?"

"Ryan…"

"This is war, Theo! I am not the most important part of this war!"

"Ryan, look out!"

Behind me, I heard the cock of a rifle. Slowly, I turned to find a Viet Cong soldier, spitting on the floor. His eyes were mournful as he pointed the gun at my chest, those irises wistful, unamused.

I didn't have time to raise my gun. Didn't have time to defend myself. I don't think I could, even if I wanted to. So, I stared the barrel down, standing my ground. I would heal, no matter what, I would always heal. It was my only curse, after all, my one superpower against the world...

Bam!

When the shot fired, someone shoved me to the ground. *No.*

And above me, Theo caught my shot square in the palm of his hand. And another. And another, the bullets striking him like the mannequins on the shooting range.

Idiot.

I shot the man in the shoulder. He yowled as he struck the foliage with a loud thud—but he would live. My aim made sure that he would live, to remember what he did. Within me, the blood in my ears hissed. He should be glad that I didn't kill him.

I surveyed the remains of the battlefield, the jungle floor littered with dead men and rifles. The surviving ambushers had already retreated, and the remaining American soldiers stumbled from their hiding spots and laid there, wounded, weeping on the floor.

So much destruction...

But I didn't even know what we were fighting for.

Sucking in a breath, I turned to Theo.

His mangled arm laid limp at his side, uniform ripped and bloodied, cropped hair stained with the jungle's debris. But even as his tears wiped the dirt from his cheeks, he laughed as if it was the funniest thing in the world. Throwing my rifle aside, I sat cross-legged before him, gingerly propping his head up on my knee. Even with three weeks of first aid, they never taught us how to stop the bleeding of five bullet wounds. In a panicked frenzy, I shucked off my jacket, fashioning it around his hand like a tourniquet.

Five seconds later, his gut-wrenching screams forced me

to remove the fabric.

I could do nothing—I could do nothing as I watched him laugh on the floor, blood pouring from his bullet wounds like a waterfall, as he waited to die.

My eyes fogged, but I held in the tears, if only for his sake. "You may be smart, Theo," I croaked, "but you are the biggest idiot I know."

"I saved your life, man," he said, wincing as his wicked laughter grew into a cough. "You were going to die."

I gasped in a breath. "I wasn't going to die."

"Yes, you were Ryan. He had a straight shot"

Water stung behind my eyes. "I wasn't going to die, Theo."

"Man, that guy was going to shoot you in the chest. . ."

"I'm immortal, Theodore," I whispered, my voice like sandpaper. "I can't die."

The words hung in the air, clinging to my skin like the muggy fog.

Theo's laughter stopped. For a moment he stared, and through his glassy eyes, I could see his mind whirring a million miles an hour. Then, he cracked a grin. "Sorry, I think the blood loss is screwing with my brain. For some reason, I thought you just—"

"Ten years ago," I said, "I tried to commit suicide by jumping out of a five-story building. I... I broke all of my bones—I should've died—but a few days later I woke up in the hospital with nothing but a couple of bruises."

I think for the first time in his life, Theo was stunned into silence.

Finally, he asked: "How old are you?"

"Sixteen hundred years old."

An odd look stuck there on his face; not one of guilt or

sorrow, but of something else.

Awe.

He stared up at the canopy, watching the sun stream through the gargantuan leaves. The soft glow cast a warm ambiance on his ever-paling face. "Well, shit."

The buzzing of the yawning jungle swallowed our silence. Though Theo concealed his pain well, sweat gathered at his brow, and he wheezed as the adrenaline begun to wear off.

I inspected his maimed arm—he would have to get it amputated, I thought—and despite every restraint holding me back, the tears began to fall, hissing in the air before they could land on his face. "I'm so sorry, Theo."

Distantly, I heard the rustling of leaves and the calling of stern voices. American soldiers, coming to collect the fallen.

"I still would've done it, you know," he gasped.

"What do you mean?"

He grinned again, but it's strained behind the grimace of his agony. "Even if I'd known you were immortal, I still would've done it."

"Why?"

Commanders and medics burst through the leaves, picking through the dead and tending to the wounded. Distantly, men called to the two of us, but in the moment neither of us heard them.

"Because I'm your friend," he said, smirking with trembling lips, "and friends save each other from pain."

I stared at that dirtied face, the man that had never shied away from the truth.

"You truly are an idiot."

"Maybe I am," he shrugged, "But you would've done the same for me."

A medic came running over, disinfectant readied in one

hand and gauze in the other. With one glance at Theo's arm, he cringed: "We're going to have to fix you up at camp. Carry him back, will ya?"

And then he left us to tend to the next fallen man.

Theo watched at the medic's receding back. "Now enough with the sappiness. Please carry me back before I gnaw my arm off myself."

I grinned, the salt of my tears stinging my cheeks. "You bastard."

Turns out the military training paid off; I hardly broke a sweat as I hauled ass back to camp, Theo half-conscious in my arms.

. . .

I inhale, sharply. Exhale.

"Bad?" Theo asks.

I grasp for words, the scar tissue of my heart pulsating with the prospect of another bleed out. Bracing myself against the window, I release a gargled gasp.

But I didn't look away.

I hadn't noticed the tubes they've stuck through his papery skin, stapled together with grotesque scars. Veins tangle on the surface of his hands like telephone wires, extending up to outline his frail form. His bald, freckled scalp contains mere wisps of gray hair, sticking out every which way. The shingles, like a burn, crawl up his un-amputated arm, disappear beneath the sleeve of his oversized "Ray's Senior Center" t-shirt. He looks like some frog or riverland creature, climbing out from the bog with outlandish skin coloring, piercing eyes slit beneath the folds of marred flesh, and cheeks like a vast cavern in the hollow of his face. Since the last time I looked at him—really looked at him, just over ten years ago when he began his metamorphosis—age had swallowed him through the pits of Hell and back.

The golden hair boy I'd fostered eternal comradery with—even as we drifted apart in the last decade. Who jumped between me and a bullet, who lost an arm to save a life that never needed to be saved. Who carried me from loneliness even when he didn't have the arm strength for it.

Who sits in his goddamn wheelchair, watching birds from his window and waiting to die.

"Theo…"

He shrugs as if his deterioration were nothing in the world. "You look exactly the same."

His voice didn't belong in that body.

"I wish I could say the same."

His half-toothed grin never left, plastered on the face that no longer belonged to the soul beneath. "You know how much time I have left?"

I shake my head. "A year?"

He shakes his head in return. "A month."

I feel his words lodge themselves into my ribcage. "A month."

He nods quietly. "A month."

Silence ebbs away at the room, a delusive phantom gliding through the air in aimless circles. "I think you're going to Heaven," I finally manage to say.

"And what makes you think that Heaven exists?"

"I just…have a feeling."

He sighs, remembering for the first time the fatigue that drags down his bones. "Try not to forget me. The old me."

I rest my hand on his remaining brittle shoulder, feeling desperately for the strength that used to radiate from him. "I wish I could forget. It would make the rest of my life easier."

He snorts. "Imagine it. Little old me, burning forever in the subconscious of an immortal's mind. I'll practically be a legend."

My vision blurs; I blink it away. Startled by the sad twang in my heart, I begin meandering towards the door. "If you're gonna be such a pain in the ass about it, you know the legend can always change."

"Maybe, maybe not," he sighs. The IV bag drapes over him like a frail, broken tree. "But at least it's something."

I stop by the door, glancing back at the silhouette of him, the crumbled sack of bones crippled before the light of the window. Looking, almost for a moment, in a way I'd never seen him. At peace. Serene, despite the horrors of PTSD that still clash through his chest. As if the roaring wolves and slamming grenades in his soul had gone utterly, utterly silent...

He never married because of the war. Never had kids, grandkids. The ghosts shook him so bad he couldn't ever go back home to face his father. Besides a couple of other friends, Theo just had me. He never lived out his dreams, never put his good brain to use. Just slowly, ever slowly, wilted away.

He spent his life fighting what he encountered in Nam.

And for him, it seemed like that was enough.

"They tell me my mind's gonna start deteriorating next week," he rasps.

I pause. "Theo…"

"Perhaps, for now, this is goodbye," he whispers, and without seeing him I can feel his eyes draping closed. "But I'll always remember you, man. Even when fate keeps us apart."

"Theo…"

But his snores sound quietly like a baby from the

wheelchair. Something ignorant, innocent, untainted by the colors of whatever came before. His death would've been the beginning of something new, waking up in the Gold Oasis as an angel in Heaven.

And he wouldn't even end up there.

I leave the room before the first tear strikes the ground.

I stroll through the hallways, past the rooms of the forgotten. Every step, another burden, another reminder that the pain never ends, that it streams through life like blood in a vein, clotting it until the artery begins to die. I trace my fingers against every door I pass, a gentle reminder that it'll all be over soon.

I'll make sure that it all ends soon.

I reach the reception, the woman still hacking away at the keyboard. Curious, I walk up to her desk.

"Why?" I ask her.

She peers up from behind her computer. "Why what?"

"Why?" I repeat. "Why would you waste your time sitting here, when there's a whole world out there for you to explore? Was there nothing else? No other thing that could give you pleasure?"

Her lips play on a smile. "I like it here."

"How could you like it here?" My voice rings out in a desperate cry. "When there are people here on their last breaths? When you're trapped here, watching them die?"

"I'm not watching them die," she says. "I'm letting them live their last days as happy as they can be."

"But what about your life?" I yell. "What about your own memories? What if you were to die tomorrow, then? In a week? Would you be happy knowing that this is how you decided to spend your last days on Earth?"

She pushes back from her desk for a second. Pondering, her slim typist hands rest thoughtfully on her chin like a marionette. She stays in this position as she whispers on a breath of quiet air, "Yes."

I'm taken aback, my hands unclenching. Without another word, she rests her hands back onto her keyboard and types. I can only watch her.

This woman plays life's game like a piano, turning the incomprehensible notes into something beautiful. Somber in sound, yet gorgeous all the same.

"What are you writing?" I ask.

Her lips crack, hands hovering over the keys. "A novel."

I shake my head, chuckling. "What a fascinating person you are."

And I turn on my heel, my boots the only signs of life trailing me as I enter back into the realm of the living. The realm of the living, the one that is ever dying like the old men and women in the senior home.

Like Theo. Like the receptionist. All of them.

And they don't even seem to care.

Picnic Blanket Dress

A SHORT STORY

I don't remember my childhood. Like a mirage of stress-free, naive fog, it emerges in my mind like a half-remembered dream that never really existed.

I don't remember when Mom had taken it, the photograph, crouched in the cheap Hallmark frame on the chipped coffee table. Don't remember, exactly, why my parents had brought three-year-old me to the park that day, capturing it timelessly in the photo. Only that it happened, and now the frame sits on our living room table among the essays and loose report cards I've carelessly dumped over it.

In the photograph, I sit on a park bench in a hideous picnic blanket dress while gripping a crumbling cookie in my chubby hands. I beam lazily into the camera, loose crumbs shoved between the cracks of my baby teeth. It looks like a stock photo of any other kid on any other bench in a frilly, little outfit. But in my parents' mind, it is the Marilyn Monroe of my distant childhood.

Iconic, they like to call it. A classic.

Sometimes I worry that they forgot the girl in the photographs decided to grow up. That she now only exists in nostalgic memory.

Now I'm sixteen, and I swear that without the photos, I would be convinced that my childhood didn't happen at all.

I sit perched on the edge of a park bench, the park bench in my childhood stock photo. I overlook the spring-scented hill I played on for the majority of my unremembered elementary school years. But instead of a cookie, a textbook on the "Wonders of World History" lies docile on its spine in my lap, and around me, notes of all shapes and sizes sway limply underneath the pencils I've strategically placed as paperweights. Above me, the sun kisses my neck, wrapping me in its embrace, trying to coax me to enjoy the day. The sweet, sultry air twists my heart into a knot, at the nostalgia my body aches to relive.

Teenage movies got it wrong; my life doesn't feel like it's being captured in a polaroid. Instead, my days seem to erode into an amorphous gray lump, with no real beginning and no foreseeable end.

I force my face back to the page, squinting at the small black lettering of the textbook. I'd been studying for the better part of three weeks, and my eyes crawl along the ancient civilization of Mesopotamia as I struggle against the exhaustion forcing me to sleep. Plugged into my headphones, blasting corny pop-rock, I uncap my highlighter with my mouth and underline.

A few feet away, a father tosses a wiffle ball to his young daughter's red plastic bat. For a three-year-old girl, her swing is remarkable, and as she makes contact the ball comes sailing towards me across the field.

I grin grimly, remembering a time when my dad used to do the same thing. (Though if he was here, he would insist I was much better at my age.)

I turn my undivided attention back towards the textbook, my eyes glazed from reading about the Epic of Gilgamesh. I grab for the highlighter in my mouth, but the pen slips before

I get a firm grip, and it twirls through the air before landing on the ground.

I reach for it in the damp grass, but a small hand beats me to it. A little girl, smiling wildly with a gapped tooth smile and a wiffle ball gripped in her hand, extends the neon pen back to me.

"Thank you," I smile, letting her drop it into my palm.

"Whatcha doing?" she asks, peering with curious eyes at the textbook.

"I'm doing my homework," I point to the highlights I've marked incoherently on the page, "and it was such a nice day that I just had to come outside."

She purses her small lips. "That's boring."

I let out a small, stale chuckle. "It's called growing up."

Her arms cross, and she stomps her flip flop on the grass. "Well, then I'm not going to grow up."

Then she runs off to her dad, and I'm left watching her shoes leave imprints in the flattened grass, not yet heavy with adulthood's phantom.

Numb to her words.

A mild breeze picks up, billowing my hair up in tendrils of disarray. The words on the page begin to blur, and my mind drifts to the childhood I lost. To the world without the stress-induced tears. To the happy little girl that only my parents remember. The spring wind howls, the papers whistling underneath the strain of their pencils, but even still they hold strong.

I look down at the chapters upon chapters of history overriding the actual history of my past.

What's the point, if the only life I remember makes me absolutely miserable?

A mighty gust of wind, great and sweet and determined,

bristles the blossoming tree leaves, the dewy grass, whispering something incomprehensible in my ear. It tickles my skin, stirring up the fuzzy memories of childhood. My childhood. The thought of it loosens the knot of tension in my gut, releasing a gasp of laughter so genuine I take myself by surprise.

Oh, but it feels so, so good.

So, I can't help but giggle, to laugh with unrestrained glee, as the wonderful wind overcomes the strength of my pencils, sending my hundreds of notes spiraling, like a kaleidoscope of monarchs, into the sky. Higher, rising above the stratosphere, it seems, escaping the claws of humanity.

And I can't even be mad; I wouldn't stop laughing, couldn't stop. Because if I stopped, I would forget the memory of my childhood that hits me like a bright red plastic bat to the face. Of the forgotten memory in the photograph, when, finally, I remember.

It was my third birthday, and all I had asked for was a chocolate chip cookie.

I look across the hills, at the scattered papers lying there, static on the fields. Dying there, like the sudden burst of ecstasy in my heart.

The winds subdue, and I'm shoved back to stone-cold reality.

We are all destined to grow up, to lose the joy of that girl gone forever in the picnic blanket dress.

But despite it all, I smile, meandering across the grass to gather my notes—two thousand years of history, stacked up in a bundle between my arms. The little girl slaps another ball into the sky, sailing at unbelievable height before landing at my feet.

She stumbles over her flip flops as she comes over to

gather it. I pick it up, handing it back to her.

"Thank you," she pants, grasping it with her grubby hands. "Are you still doing your boring homework?"

I tilt my head towards the sun, welcoming the warmth of the spring. "No," I say. "There's something else I want to do instead."

"Oh yeah? What's that?"

I look at her with a childish grin. "I want to have a picnic."

Not Like the Eighties

A SHORT STORY

Beatrice hadn't always been so simple. She hadn't always limited herself to two Thin Mints a day, drank half a glass of Manischewitz before bed, and wore red sweaters during the spring. Working at the library tends to make people as stuffy as the books they carry, and as for Beatrice, she hadn't been spared.

She had Ashkenazi in her blood. When her grandfather fled from Poland three years before the Second World War, she always thought that the bloodline made her stronger, that the Eastern European grit penetrated the murky crevices of her genetically brilliant mind, that perhaps—perhaps—she was as strong as Grandfather.

Of course, that's precisely how she ended up as a librarian.

Even since her thirtieth birthday, her life has spiraled into a slow, cold rhythm. No longer did her husband kiss her when she went out for work. At the library, paperwork drowned the thrill of the knowledge around her—who knew the library needed so much filing? Even with her Pilates classes, which provide her with a much-needed endorphin rush, nothing gave her solace in the wake of her routine.

Routine. When did her life become so routine? Turns out that once you graduate from UCSD with a bachelor's in English studies you get all the jobs that no one of any lesser intellect stands to do. After all, life just becomes one long circle of routines: work, sleep, eat, stretch, defecate, repeat. And they expect you to do that, all for the best of thirty-five years (thirty-five, no that seems too long, it couldn't be that long) until you retire, move to some foreign Eastern country, and live out the rest of your days with your husband who's fallen out of love with you, but it doesn't matter because you both develop dementia and die.

All roads lead to death, it seems

These were the thoughts that swam through Bea's head that afternoon, mindlessly shuffling paperwork and staring intently at the monitor before her. She fixes the glasses strap fastened behind the strands of her ever-deflating ring of curls. Stretching her crackling legs beneath the desk, she observes the ceiling, white and rimmed with light fixtures. It all seems so claustrophobic, with the walls and the ceiling so close to the top of her frail head. But after fifty-seven years she almost doesn't mind the walls confining her. It's just there, a box Bea gave up on trying to escape...

A man in grey sweatpants confronts her then, dumbly scratching his thick head of brown hair, wondering where the book checkout is. Startled, she turns her attention to him, cursing him out about the automatic book scanner fifty feet to his right. In an apologetic shrug, he shuffles away, turning back to look at the woman and wondering what the hell her deal was. And why was she wearing a sweater in April?

Her gaze returns to the ceiling, sighing.

At one point in her life, she had been magnificent. Back in the eighties, where big hair and drugstore eyeshadow were all the rage, where leg warmers were in fashion and she didn't have to be judged for being so goddamn cold all the time. Where her metabolism still existed and love was reckless and she was reading the works of Jane Austen in her free time right after her volunteer job at the library, taking weekly trips down to the roller rink with the Lovecraft-obsessed boy. Back in the time of her life, she dreamed of a world where she could escape the grasp of humanity with the love of her life somewhere far, far away.

No parents, no responsibility, just her and the boy who asked her to marry him.

Now, look where their relationship is now.

How the times change.

She glances back at the monitor, at the one hundred eight emails left unread. She looks at the clock, then back at the monitor, then up at the ceiling. This was her life now, a stuffy librarian who'd fallen from her prime.

Slowly, she lifts the sleeve of her atrocious red sweater, tracing the lines of her tattoo in the crease of her elbow. A sun, carved there forever when she was in Bali on the eve of her thirtieth birthday.

It was a toast to new beginnings. To love. To life.

To Bea, love and life seemed very far away.

Part 4:

Home Sweet Home

Giants in the Sky

A SHORT STORY

The ancient cavern in the jungle is the corpse of a giant, its jaw unhinged to expose a corral of cavities and golden teeth. Moss sprouts from the innards, spilling from the carcass and overgrown with stretching trees. The humidity of Costa Rica haunts the fauna—save for the mosquitos that enjoy the daily circus of nipping at ignorant tourists—and the rain excites the flora, thriving from the guts of the wayward giant.

A jungle of green is what remains of the beast. But what came before lives on only as a mystery.

The natives tell a story of the hundred-meter men who used to roam with the dinosaurs. These men were quite curious creatures, for they look more like enormous mice than men. Large, hairy beings with two sets of unfashionably large buck teeth, claws like fingers, sniveling snouts, overgrown toenails protruding from wrinkled feet. They could stomp out the life of a dinosaur with a well-placed kick or a welted rock. Compared to the dinosaurs who lived amongst them, the giants were gods. That's what the indigenous people remember them as, anyways.

And they died, without anything but their wilted bones to mark that they existed at all.

But I remember them, saw them with my own eyes. I remember, for I lived among them as a ghost of nature, watching these magnificent beasts—the giants in the sky.

No, they weren't gods. They were spirits of Earth, their average minds conjuring new ways to rearrange the flowers and the trees below. Their heads could graze the clouds, yes, but no sooner were they tall were their dense heads quick to tip them over. If anything, the giants have proved to be a nuisance in the story of evolution, clumsy beings only good for tripping over their overgrown feet.

They did, however, had a fascinating fixation with nature.

I suppose that was part of their curse.

Because though they loved the world around them, they would no sooner destroy it. They would pluck entire ecosystems from the ground like dandelions, depositing them some one hundred meters away, floating in the ocean or in the heart of the desert. Flora and fauna alike, nothing was safe from the terrors of the giant's touch.

And at nights, beneath their makeshift bungalows, you could hear them moaning, mourning the loss of the nature they could only destroy.

So perhaps it was fitting that they became the thing they so dearly desired.

For as the meteors struck the earth and as the giants tripped over their massive paws for perhaps the last time, I watched the emergence of a new life among the brambles of the dying world. Rodents scurried underneath the cooler, softer earth, hiding underneath their taller, deader brethren. As one, the mice emerged from the soil, a rebirth from the monsters they had been born. And with time, even as the animals around them mutated, the rats stayed relatively the same, savoring every moment upon the ground.

They enjoyed the land for their ancestors that could not.

Meanwhile, the giants fertilized the soil, their strong bones decomposing in the Earth. They created the jungle, animating it with their undying spirit. In the underbrush, they formed a Heaven for their grandchildren, the mice, and all the other mammals hiding from the predators of the new world.

The ancestors and the living, combined as one, dwelling in the same region for all of eternity.

Thriving for nature. The sweet and solemn nature.

So, walk through the jungle, my friends, and witness the spirits of creation at work again.

The King

A SHORT STORY

No one has seen the King for twenty-one days.

All is normal, seems normal; the subjects seek common courtesy, criminals seek to sink their own morality. The knights still roam castle grounds, the chambermaids still take out what little wash is left of the royal household—the Queen and her four children. Horses nicker proudly as they parade the town in groups of threes with jesters and dancers in tow, displaying the white and green banners of the still very-much-sovereign Majesty.

But at night in her bedroom chamber, wearing nothing but her scandalous nightgown and fear on her face, the Queen asks her senior advisor what they must do. Not one of her subjects can know the secrets about the unstable grounds of the kingdom, for their lies will spread in the streets like a deadly disease, and then what? Anarchy? Chaos? She buries her face in her hands.

The advisor tries to reassure her, patting her awkwardly on the shoulder. "They will not know. We will make sure of it."

And indeed they made sure of it, for even for the children of the royal family didn't know what was wrong.

"Where's Father?" asks the youngest of the four, a five-year-old girl with pigtails and an ego inflated like party balloons.

"Does it matter right now, princess?" the governess

hushes her, straightening the girl's petticoats and guiding her back to her studies. "Besides, if he's gone, does that mean that your focus shall suffer, too?"

And that was that.

The Queen glances out the window of her study's tower, her curls quivering nervously in the crisp Autumn morning. To her advisor, she whispers, "any news?"

"Only that the King's disappeared for twenty-one days now, Highness."

Her slow exhale seems to rumble the stones of the gloomy castle. "Shall we send out more troops."

"Highness, we've sent nearly half our soldiers..."

"That was not a question, Thomas."

In the forest, troops indeed have been sent by the thousands upon the Queen's request. A commander bolsters himself to his horse, distributing frantic words to his subordinates.

"The future of the kingdom rests in ye grubby paws!"

So they all searched frantically, without a single idea of what they might be looking for.

All in vain, really. For no one truly knows what happened to him, the King. Just one day, his horse had been absent from the stables, and with it three thousand golden coins from his underground chamber. Such a shame, too, for he had won over everyone's heart, a beacon of kindness and strength for all those who knew him—the aristocracy and ordinary folk alike.

Would you die to know where your Father went, little girl? Had your eyes not been glued to your musty princess textbooks, perhaps you might be able to put some of your deduction skills to use. And what about you, Queen? Has your desperation blinded you so much that you forgot to look in the one place you'd never expect? Knights, commanders, chambermaids, civilians, would you understand that your king was neither murdered nor kidnapped nor bribed nor bored?

Would any of you believe that he was trying to run away?

Once a month, the aristocracy of the kingdom gather in the ballroom of the luxurious castle, transported in their chariots of varying shades of gold and silver. Princesses and duchesses dance in gowns sewn from what's 'in season'. Dukes and knights gawk at the beautiful women while laughing aimlessly at the same retold stories. Servants bustle with steaming platters and bubbling champagne, lurking like black shadows trailing the glistening sheen of the rich. In a corner, musicians weave music through the delightful air of the party, caressing the guests with comfort. The only thing the aristocrats must worry about is themselves and the innate pleasures of the life they've been born into.

And atop it all, sitting on a throne sculpted of the purest gold, the King always sipped his wine as the illusions of perfection sang to his guests. Always grimacing at the pure insanity of it all.

There were eight more days before the monthly party. Eight more days before everyone would know about the vanishing King.

Nearing upon the end of the twenty-first moon, still, no one has seen him. Among the few treasonous servants who knew, the speculations of his disappearance bordered on absurdity: seduced by a gypsy, haunted by the ghost of his dead father, consumed with the desire for adventure.

The answer might then disappoint you. For on the town's outskirts, a mid-thirties man watches the sun set over the looming castle. Rubbing the thick stubble on his chin, he shades his sun-worn eyes with the palm of a newly blistered hand. In the distance, a woman calls him to dinner.

"Coming," he says.

He sticks the ax head into a stump, where it will wait obediently for him until his return. With an unrestrained grin, wiping his filthy hands on the newly-worn lapel of his tunic, he turns towards the sound.

A Trip Down to Heaven

ONE DAY

Back and forth, I pace, back and forth and back and forth and
back and forth and…

December 25.

I can't sleep. For three days I haven't been able to sleep…

I glance at my watch, the anxiety rolling a knot in my gut.

Three in the morning…three more hours until…

I bend over myself, folding into a fetal ball on the kitchen
floor. I've put a disc on the vinyl player, and I hear Elvis
Presley step up to the mic, growling slyly about his blue suede
shoes.

Out of all the ninety-five vinyl records in my apartment,
it seems only fitting that Elvis would be the one to take me out
of my misery.

I stare up at the ceiling—the low, plaster ceiling,
threatening me with suffocation.

Isn't this what I wanted? To have it all crashing down
around me?

I lay on my back in the kitchen. The tile cools the sizzling
skin on my neck. The flickering lightbulb fixed into the ceiling
blinks curiously down at me, watching, waiting to see what I
do next.

I chuckle softly to myself.

What does Jeremiel think of me now?

How can time cripple you so much, sucking you into

such debilitating silence? Over the years, I've gotten good at stilling my parasympathetic nervous system. Now, I can hardly suck down a normal breath, succumbing instead to the trepidation of death

With strained effort, I sit up, propping my head against the cabinet.

You'd think I plan for this day, to know what I would do in my last hours. Get ice cream, memorize the clouds, listen to my favorite Symphony by Beethoven (the 9th, obviously). But how can you plan the perfect last day? The last week, even? It happens, and all the while you're only worried about impending doom. After my encounter with Theo, I've spent the majority of the past two days on the floor, the stuttering of my heart silencing me into helpless oblivion.

Sometimes I think it'd be better to not know the world was ending at all.

But Jeri didn't have to tell me about the meteor. He could've let me live the way I was living—in cold monotony for the final week of my life. Perhaps he thought I would take the bribe to save the world, perhaps he knew I would spend the last week in sheer panic.

But he told me, understanding that, for some reason, it was better for me to know than to live in blissful ignorance.

He gave me the choice to live a better life.

And I realize that I wasn't going to waste it.

"Come on!" I shove myself to my feet, wobbling from the bitter migraine that's begun in my temples. A plan formulates in my mind, festering like a parasite.

This is not how I'm going to leave the Earth. Not like this.

I know, at least for now, what to do.

I grab an ancient coat from my dresser—when tweed

was the height of fashion—and barge out the door, leaving the keys in the living room and Elvis spinning out on the record player.

. . .

It's three-fifteen when I trek down the frigid avenues of New York City, eyes darting between my watch and the moon. Compulsively, I watch the time. As if it were sand in an hourglass, I could never really be sure how fast it was falling until the final grain struck the bottom, ending a surefire fate.

So I walk, and I check.

It's three-twenty when I wind up at the Catholic Church, grappling at the iron bars in the front. I bang at the lock. I kick the gate. It doesn't budge. Fuming, I take a bit of rock on the sidewalk and chuck it at the door.

I don't notice when Jeremiel appears at my side until he begins to speak. "You look like you're doing well."

"Shut up," I mutter.

His presence emanates warmth in the crisp cold of New York Christmas. "Oh, the mighty immortal bastard, slipping from sanity in his last few hours of existence."

"Shut up."

"I truly pity you, my friend. I mean, this is what you wanted, right? To live in the finite moment, knowing that, at last, it would end—"

"Of course, this is what I wanted!" I cry. The bars rattle with another one of my futile kicks. "And I still want it! I've always wanted it!"

I clutch my arms, shivering. When did it get so cold? "I just...you wouldn't understand. I don't even understand. I thought I would understand. But turns out you can't conceptualize death until it's pointing the barrel of its gun at you, and no matter how much I tell myself otherwise, deep down I'm afraid. I've spent so long hoping that there would be a day that I wouldn't exist, and all of a sudden, it's here and...I didn't live long enough to ever feel ready for that."

Jeremiel and I stand there, mute, watching the clouds drift over the cross of the church, waltzing in the wind. Taking in the utter silence of the sad, solemn serenade of the night, singing its song in resignation for what's to come.

Jeri gives me a sidelong glance, patting me tightly on the shoulder. Sighing, I turn towards the streets, looking up at the manmade trees of the concrete jungle.

"What now?" he asks me.

I close my eyes, heavy with the exhaustion of the past week. I want to succumb to sleep, to have someone tuck me in and watch me slumber soundly as the meteor streaks the sky. But I couldn't do that—what an anticlimactic end to the upward climb of one thousand six hundred ninety-four years.

I open my eyes, checking the time. Three-thirty. "I think I know where I need to go."

. . .

I don't remember my birth.

I vaguely remember my childhood.

I remember my birth name: Alexander. What a crap name.

I remember the normalcy of my youth, my more than ordinary parents—both of whom were poor merchants during the Roman Empire. We would travel for days on end, sailing through the Mediterranean Sea.

I remember Rome, the empire it had been, the brilliance

of both the smooth, sensational language and hand-crafted goods piquing my youthful curiosity. Neither of my parents remembered the exact day of my birthday—sometime in March—but during that month I was allowed to pick out one thing from the marketplace (and immediately lose it, because I was a five-year-old with no sense of responsibility).

Being the son of two traveling merchants, I practically lived on that ship. I never settled down, never befriended anyone my age, only my assertive parents and the people that they sold to. I remember the long, lazy days on the ship when my father would review trade routes on age-stained maps. I would be the one responsible for making sure the lamp didn't go out.

It was a life of simplicity, marked by long voyages and occasional seasickness and the reckless, adolescent desire to be more than what the meager world had to offer.

All was normal until I stopped aging at twenty-one.

Obviously, it took a while to realize. As my parents grew older, I took up the trade, buying herbs from doctors whenever they began to fall ill and whenever I could afford it. My mother died when she was forty-five; it was the first of thousands of deaths I would experience in my lifetime. When my father died a year later, just on the cusp of my twenty-eighth birthday, I discovered how utterly alone I truly was.

But I knew no other life than what my parents had shown me. And besides, I lost that youthful desire for success a long time ago. So I awaited death like a friend, shuttling goods across the Mediterranean and watching the days fly before my eyes. Never loving, never dreaming, never living.

It was the new year of my one hundredth birthday when I remember watching myself in the Mediterranean waters and finally embracing my supposed immortality.

Of course, I'd long suspected that this was the case. My customers began dying out, and their sons replaced them, followed by their grandsons. Between days at the marketplace and out at sea, I would observe my reflection in the still pools of the ocean— rumpled hair, brown unblemished skin, youthful cheeks, boyish lips—and then I'd watch my eyes, my protruding hazel eyes. They were the only thing that ever seemed to age, them and the hollow black eyebags underneath.

I was immortal. An anomaly. A freak of nature.

And I hated it.

I made myself unexceptional, indistinguishable from the crowds. No one, except perhaps my scarce crew of five men, ever seemed to notice the undying merchant boy selling them their wares.

By the time the Roman Empire fell in 476 AD, I was one hundred fifty-nine years old.

. . .

It is five o'clock when I finish climbing up the twenty flights of stairs and onto the roof the old apartment that Jeri and I used to share. The best view of New York City.

Scattered snowflakes twirl in the early morning wind, performing a poorly rehearsed ballet on their way down, down, down to the city floor. Even before the presence of the sun, the sky glows hazy, igniting in a purplish hue.

Breathless, I inhale with gut-wrenching gulps, and the cold consolidates my exhales into eerie white vapor, clouding around my head. I lost all of my physical strength from the Vietnam War, and my legs wobble like wet noodles, shaking beneath the throbbing in my fearful heart.

One hour to go.

Jeremiel materializes beside me, straightening the cuffs of his blinding suit. "I'm genuinely impressed you could run five miles that fast."

I peel the tweed from my sweaty arms, bunching it into a cloth lump in my hands. "I could be worse."

"Trust me, you have been worse."

I slap his shoulder. "Shut up."

Chuckling, he walks across the rooftop towards the ledge. "Back where we started."

I nod, walking over to the edge towards him. "And nothing has changed."

Jeri leans over the edge, wings outstretched to catch him if he falls. For a moment, he bows into the wind, basking in it. I join him, embracing the chill in my extended arms, and goosebumps prickle along my sickly skin. It allowed me, for a too-brief moment, to escape the grasp of my fleeting reality.

Finally, he stands back, looking down at the empty streets. "It's quite sad."

"What is?" I muse, gesturing towards the city. "Is it because we're all going to die in an hour? Or because you're going to miss Earth?"

He purses his lips, shaking his head. "It's Christmas."

My favorite holiday.

"Huh." I gaze back at the skyline. "I guess it is."

The city pulsates with the prospect of life, golden trinkets and fairy lights hanging over every street corner, flickering dully against the yellow street lamps. In their apartments, almost everyone sleeps peacefully, awaiting the sunrise to begin the happiest day of the year. In the most glamorous city in the world, on the best day in the Western hemisphere, no one knew the fate waiting for them. I sit on the ledge, letting my legs dangle over the sides.

"And I can't even enjoy it," I murmur.

. . .

Fifteen minutes.

I shiver as the snow trickles down heavier around us. My body trembles not from the cold outside, but rather from the numb that's overtaken me. I squeeze my arms tightly to my chest, watching the dawning horizon slowly erupt before my eyes.

All the while, Jeremiel doesn't leave my side. Silent, he waits patiently with me for the sunrise of a lifetime. Unsure of what to say, uncertain of what conversation might be right for this moment, he just sits there with me.

Watching, and waiting.

My stomach grumbles. I didn't even have the chance to have a last meal. What would my last meal even be? Since being in America, I could only stomach the foods from my past. (McDonald's hamburgers, forget about it—the cheese is the yellow of toxic sludge.) Maybe gelato? But it's Christmas day; I don't want a frozen dessert when the Earth can make it outside my front door. Right now, I'm craving a cranberry muffin with oolong tea, baked French fries and grilled squash, a falafel and Italian pizza, tiramisu and goulash. Perhaps if I had another day...another year...

I glance down at my watch. Ten minutes.

"Shit!" I pound my fists into the stone. Jeremiel jumps, shoving me in the shoulder.

"My God!" he sighs, exasperated. "What's wrong?"

"I—" I inhale, burying my face in my hands. "I just wish I had more time!"

"You still can!" he gestures at the sky, the sun not yet

over the horizon. "It's not too late!"

"I told you Jeri! I can't keep living like this!" I breathe. "This is my way out! This is my lifeline, and if I don't take it now, I…"

I groan, ruffling my hair with twitching fingers. "I'd rather die than to keep on like this."

Jeremiel blinks, and suddenly the backs of his manicured hands seem all too interesting.

"I know," he says. "I know.

. . .

For the entirety of my life, I sailed the world in search of meaning.

I had a few lovers, never marrying, never settling.

I traveled to all parts of the Eastern hemisphere, selling my wares in whatever place would take them.

Aboard my merchant ship, then pirate ship, then fishing ship, I made (and lost) friends that I don't even remember the names of anymore.

I don't remember specific days, only years, decades, when business was good and I could afford simple luxuries—food, hotel rooms, women. Then I would go to bed, wake up, and do everything all over again.

Forever stuck in time's loop.

And through it all, I survived.

Hatefully, and awfully, survived.

. . .

Five minutes.

My knee trembles, shaking so badly I have to brace it

down with my elbows.

The sun begins its upwards ascent, propelling itself into the sky. Jeremiel gasps softly; it takes all my willpower not to do the same.

For a doomsday sunrise, God did a spectacular job.

The lustrous sky glows amber as the sun pushes itself higher, higher from behind the buildings. Above, the dwindling black of nighttime shines purple, then deep blue, as the glorious sun leeches the night of its darkness into a warm ambiance of Heavenly light.

I laugh, a weary sound in my chest. "It's been a good run, hasn't it?"

Jeremiel shrugs. "I've been an angel for the past seventy years. I think my run ended a long time ago."

The sun soars higher into the air, preparing for its daily feat.

Four minutes.

"Do you know how much you hurt me, Jeri?"

"You jumped out a window for me."

The statement is offhand, but the words ache, like a bruise on his soul.

"You know what I mean."

He sighs. "Look, I... human suffering is inevitable. It doesn't matter how good or bad you are. You will suffer, and when you do it's the worst feeling in the world. But you brush yourself off, wipe away your tears, and you just keep going."

"I've been looking my whole life, Jeri. What if it just wasn't out there for me?"

"It always is. I found it; you can find it, too. You just have to stop caring."

Three minutes.

"You still mean the world to me," he says.

I turn to look at Jeremiel. "I don't want to hear it."

"I think you just don't want to admit that this decision doesn't just affect you."

"Yeah, well, there's no point in telling me now. You could've told me seventy years ago."

He shakes his head, the golden locks brushing his shaven chin. "Would it have mattered? You wouldn't have believed me then."

He's right. Despite the world crashing and burning around us, he's the only one that would ever understand me. The only one I dared to rely on, even when he wasn't there. No matter what, we were the only two loners in an unkind world, haunted by the infinity of a life that would never end.

"You never had to tell me," I say. "I already knew."

Two minutes.

"Did you ever decide on your name?" Jeremiel asks.

I shake my head, chuckling. "Nothing ever really stuck."

He clicks his tongue. "How strange. After sixteen hundred years the one thing you never did was choose a name you liked."

"It doesn't matter," I shrug. "No one but you is going to remember me when I'm gone."

"Maybe," he says. "But when I tell the old folk in the Gold Oasis about my life, I can't just call you my 'best friend'. Then it's like you weren't really my best friend, you know?"

I ponder for a moment. "Then I'll let you name me."

Jeri smiles. "It will be the best name the world has ever heard."

One minute.

A flash illuminates the sky. White and flaming, it leaps from space and soars like the tail of a firework down, down, down.

There it is; the end of the Earth, in the form of a dinky rocket flying from the sky.

How anticlimactic.

Jeri claps me on the back. "I'll miss you, old friend."

I nod. I want to say more—I would have said more—but my heart palpitates painfully, racing like a sprinter on the Olympic stage. This is it; this is what I've always wanted—

The sun breaches the rooftops, its tendrils leaping onto every brick and stone of the magnificent city. Even with the glowing meteor in the sky, whistling angrily on its descent, the sun overrides it, smothering the last bits of the Christmas cold. If the sun could sing at that moment, it would burst out in melodious opera, stealing the breaths of everyone willing to listen to its sweet, powerful voice.

This—this is the last sunrise on Earth.

I think of my parents, of my failed relationships, my dead friends and sea goers who I don't know the names of anymore, their faces flashing through my head in a blur. No matter how long I live, I can never forget them. No matter how hard I slam my head into a wall, their faces are imprinted into my mind. My memory is titanium: unbendable, unbreakable, unbearable.

But then I remember.

I remember the woman at the bar, the determination for hope at her tipsy fingertips. I remember the men in Temple, praying to an entity that they had no proof even existed, hoping that the world could, one day, be better. I remember Theo, who I battled alongside as a comrade and as a friend in the hopes of preserving peace and happiness in a war-torn world and an equally damaged mind.

Then I remember Jeremiel. My one true best friend. Who

left Earth in the hopes of a better life. Who I sailed the seven seas with, who I shared stories of my existence with, the women (and men) we've encountered, the places we've seen, the food we've eaten. We've spent long days out fishing, long nights out dancing, living for a brief time in the fantasy that happiness could be infinite, that there was hope that life could be like that forever.

And that's when I realize.

Hope.

It's hope.

That's what people live for, clinging onto the idea that, one day, it will get better.

And no matter how minuscule, I realize, that hope alone is worth living for.

"This needs to stop." I murmur. "Jeri, I changed my mind. I changed my mind; I don't want the world to end."

For a moment, he just stares. "And you're deciding this now?"

"Yes, I'm sorry. Please, I've made a mistake."

"My friend..."

"I've made a mistake!" my voice quivers, heart roaring in my chest. "I'm sorry. I understand now, I need you to make it—"

The world shudders, a sickening cry running down every bone in my body.

And just like that, the sand slips between my fingers.

I have run out of time.

An earthquake rumbles beneath my feet, the wind whistling like an atom bomb.

"I'm sorry, my friend," Jeri steps up onto the ledge. "You wouldn't have been able to stop it, anyway."

The wind blinds me, deafening me with its battle-cries. "What do you mean?"

His exhausted voice stops short of a sob. "You can't stop Fate. No one can. Not even God can."

Wait.

"What?"

"It was inevitable. No matter what you chose, whether it was to keep on living or to let the world die, the meteor was going to come."

"So, the offer you gave me...to save the world..."

"It was fake," he says, his voice a rasp beneath the hissing wind. "No matter what, the world was going to end."

I stare at him. "You gave me a choice between life and death. Why?"

He presses his lips into a tight line.

"Jeri, why did you give me false hope?"

Heat sears my skin, blaring like desert afternoons. Just barely, I can make out his figure, observing the skyline with a somber glare.

Finally, painfully, he turns to me and says: "I thought you would choose to save the world."

I stare at him. "Jeri..."

"I hoped that you would be able to be happy in your last moments, knowing that you chose life over death. I didn't think you would make your decision so late. I'm sorry."

"Jeri...."

He turns back towards the sun, peering at it in a sad sort of way. Opening his wings, he states to no one in particular, "to new infinities."

I grab his wing before he can fall.

"Jeremiel," I murmur, looking up into his enchanted eyes. "Thank you. For being there for me."

His grim stare light up, crystal irises watering. I pull him into an embrace. Around us, the wind threatens to rip us apart, to tear at his pristine suit and my threadbare clothes until we stand there naked before the apocalypse.

But I squeeze him tighter than I ever thought I could, because letting him go means I have to disappear forever. He throws up his wings, cocooning us in temporary utopia against the elements.

Nothing could ever rip us apart. Never again.

He pushes me back, holding me at my forearms, memorizing the lines of my face. "Don't forget about me in the Abyss," he whispers.

"I don't think that's possible."

Jeremiel grins, his tears swept away by the wind. I look down at his whitening knuckles on my forearms, unable to let go, not ever wanting to let go....

I hear the distant sound of a toppling building, ushering the world's destruction in a bone-crackling earthquake. I turn to look, and when I turn back, he's let go of my arms, unable to remove his eyes from me as he steps onto the ledge.

He raises his fingers in a two-finger salute.

"Goodbye, old friend."

I return it with wobbling fingers.

"Goodbye, Captain."

Jeremiel disappears in the air before the world explodes.

The sky fractures, the ground crackling like the skin of a

dead man in the desert. One by one, the buildings plummet—like dominos—to the streets. Eerie yellow gas rises from the ashes, swarming the city like bees, attacking the world with an unforgiving plague.

All the while, the sun sits on its perch, nonchalant. Watching.

It is beautiful; my God, I could not begin to explain how beautiful it is.

The yellow fog consumes me, climbing through my nose, ripping at my lungs. Like a lion, it claws at me, choking me, killing me from the inside out.

I stand there over the edge, unable to breathe. If I could laugh I would—wheezing at the irony of the beauty of death—but I could only produce a silent hack as I straighten my spine and salute the sun in mocking formality.

"Good game, my friend," I mouth. "Good game."

Then I jump, lost to the sound silence of Death's tranquility before I could even hit the floor.

Epilogue

Utopia

INFINITE DAYS

Date: unknown.

I am here.

A speck of dust in the cosmos. An atom brushing the surface of the universe.

In nothingness, I have a lot of time to think. Nameless, I am but a ghost in the afterlife, amidst all the other particles of beings who never made it to Heaven but weren't enough of an asshole to go down to Hell.

Maybe Theo made it down here. Maybe María made it, too, all those years ago.

My memories are my only peers, preserving my spirit in matter smaller than a molecule of air. After all, all anyone is is their memories. At least in the afterlife, people are able to keep that part of themselves.

I don't know what happened to the Earth; I don't know what happened to Jeremiel; I don't know who got to die and who kept on living.

Despite that, there is one thing I know for absolute certainty:

Finally, in my pathetic life, I am dead.

I am normal.

I am free.

And that's all I ever wanted.

Pura Vida

A SHORT STORY

I'm plagued by the agonizing screams of the rain. Like dictators demanding control from their opposition, it slams against the tile roof and spills in a waterfall upon the cement. At nights here in Costa Rica I can't sleep, too caught up in the chaos of the water banging against the windows.

I'm too used to the empty silence in suburbia, where the weather is mild and my internal nagging erodes away the quiet. Even now, with the buzzing of the water, my inner voice competes in weary competition, fighting for control of my consciousness, my mind. At least at home, the words erupt within me in violent whispers.

Never screams; the thoughts never scream like this.

Nature is filled with water, especially in Costa Rica. The roar of white-water rapids, the steaming hot springs underneath the canopy of the rainforest. The waterfalls. You can't picture the sounds of water until the silence of the outside courses it through your weary veins, shutting your thoughts into oblivion and just letting you be.

That's all nature is, after all; the state of being.

And water is but one way of cleansing, it seems. To weed out the unnatural stress of technology into the greater world of being.

They say a phrase here in Costa Rica: Pura Vida. Pure

life.

Among the canopy of trees and leaf-cutter ants and the godawful festering mosquitos, everything thrives in the jungle. Pura Vida. Pure life.

The tour guides who smile not because they have to but because they live in a place that embraces humanity through nature and love for the planet. Pura Vida. Pure life.

Every friendly handshake, genuine smile, and heckling laugh holds the promise of a wonderful world with an even brighter future.

Pure life. Simple life. Built on the scaffolding of self, not on reformation. Happiness, not conformity. Love, not tolerance.

Perhaps the rain, then, is not screaming. It's laughing. Thriving in the freedom of the glorious, glorious jungle.

Thriving in the power of simply being.

Teaching me simply,

very simply,

 to be.

Acknowledgments

To the one trip to Costa Rica that inspired it all.
To Grandpa, my editor, who embraced this challenge with
open arms and made the process so much easier.
And to Mom, Dad, and Dillon, who always make my
world that much brighter.
I love you all.

Pura Vida,
Halle

www.ingramcontent.com/pod-product-compliance
Lightning Source LLC
Chambersburg PA
CBHW020123180726
47992CB00020B/2197